The Devil's Marque

Mike Macartney

The Devil's Marque

Published by Shoot Your Eye Out Publishing
Copyright © Mike Macartney 2015
No part of this publication may be reproduced, stored in a retrieval system, or transmitted in any form or by any means whether electronic, mechanical, photocopying, recording, scanning, or otherwise, except as permitted under Sections 107 or 108 of the 1976 United States Copyright Act without the prior written permission of the publisher.

The Devil's Marque is a work of fiction. All incidents, dialogue, and characters, with the exception of historical and public figures, are products of the author's imagination and are not to be construed as real. Where historical or public figures appear, the situations, incidents, and dialogue concerning those persons are entirely fictional and are not intended to depict actual events or to change the entirely fictional nature of the work. In all other aspects, any resemblance to persons living or dead is entirely coincidental.

ISBN: 978-0-9886445-2-6 ebook
0988644526

978-0-9886445-3-3 print
0988644533

Manufactured in the United States of America

For Remo, Ian, and Cindy

CONTENTS

Acknowledgements

This book could not have been written as well as it has been without the tireless editing by Cindy Robins-Macartney. Like all good editors she was ruthless and that's what it needed.

I wish to thank Jennifer "J. J." Brown for reading the first draft and providing detailed feedback. Mark Jameson also read the draft and provided necessary suggestions, as did Steve Ulrich. This book would not be what it is without them.

I would also like to thank Mary Gustafson for the original artwork on the cover.

Introduction

This is a work of fiction. No characters are based on living people. The only references to living people are to public figures and those references are completely fictional in nature. Historical figures appear in the book, and are presented only in the context of what history says about them. James Hazen, for example, was the president of the Equitable Life Assurance Company. He really did go to France after he resigned from Equitable and 40 other companies for having a lavish costume party on the company's dime. It was the last straw for the board.

The Canton Bank of San Francisco was a real bank and the Sam Wo restaurant was a San Francisco institution for 100 years, from 1912 to 2012. As of July 2015 it is being rebuilt and will reopen under the same name in a new location.

There is no such company as Nationwide Professional Services to the author's knowledge, and the depiction of that company is completely fictional and not based on any existing or historical company. There is no McKean Mining either.

Research was done on early skyscrapers and street locations and they were used in a fictional way in the book. There is a Buddha Bar hotel in Paris.

There are historical figures used for the chapters about Reno and Las Vegas. Lincoln Fitzgerald was a real person and his depiction is based on actual events, as was Joe Conforte and Jimmy Ing. My family knew all of them in one way or another. My aunt worked at the Nevada Club for more than thirty years. Joe Conforte played pinochle in my parents' casino, the Ohio Club, where they operated the last no-limit poker games in Nevada until 1966. Jimmy Ing owned the bar behind the Ohio Club facing East Commercial Row. It had a connecting door to the Ohio Club and my mother fought with him constantly to keep the door closed and not let anybody from the bar walk through my parent's club. He finally got an order from the city and the landlord (Jack Douglas) to keep the door open. My mother closed it anyway – she had no fear.

There is an actual historical reference to a Chinese maker of gaming equipment in Silver Peak around the turn of the century. My parents had the last Farobank game in Nevada at the Ohio Club. I was told their Farobank layout (the betting platform used in the game with playing cards mounted on it) was made by a Chinese man in Tonopah early in the 20th Century. Maybe it was.

There was a real person named Lee Toy too. He worked for my parents as a shill in their poker and lo ball games. His right hand was deformed, he said from a laundry press, and he kept it in his pocket. He ate peanuts and water to save his money to gamble with, and ended up with tuberculosis in the Weimar Sanatorium in Northern California. He lived there for nine months as an indigent patient in the late 1960s. He made a lamp out of a Manzanita root there for my parents because they visited him there several times. I still have the lamp. He is long dead and probably buried in an unmarked grave somewhere around Reno. He never had a wife or children as far as I know. Maybe using his name in this book will add a little immortality to a forgotten soul, if there is such a thing.

Mike Macartney

Calliope

Mike Macartney

Chapter 1

San Francisco, California April 2014

When you have a demon draped upon your French provincial loveseat, the one with red velour stripes in the middle your living room, the double fudge chocolate chip ice cream may not suffice.

Calliope chose a special triple chocolate espresso truffle for her visitor out of the "specials" drawer in the mid-century modern armoire standing elegantly against the red upstairs living room wall.

***

Calliope made the specials, and the everydays too, from secret ingredients she ordered that arrived in simple packages with odd return address. She bought others herself in equally out of the way places nearby. The makings had once come from Calliope's great aunt Hermione. Great aunt Hermione had given Calliope her own potion book long ago for her ninth birthday, so wherever Hermione was now she was making them from memory. The girl immediately set about practicing making them herself. She experimented with noxious recipes using the exotic biological and chemical ingredients her great aunt sent, along with lots of sugar and chocolate of course, to the detriment of the atmosphere of various rooms in her family's suburban ranch house.

Great aunt Hermione always liked Calliope. They were thick as thieves when she visited. Even so Calliope did not seem at all upset when she disappeared into that filthy alley in Poughkeepsie never to be seen at the quiet little suburban house again. The strange potions book had shown up on the front stoop one morning shortly after Hermione's last visit.

June and Albert and their daughter Calliope's family home nestled under broad green leaves in the

3

perfectly normal looking little cul-de-sac. It was one of those with careful little green lawns and two cars in the driveway – unless there was a boat in one of the parking spots instead. The normal house with the normal looking Dancer family with the outgoing pudgy daughter never attracted attention until that ninth summer, when Britney Alexandra became Calliope.

The pudgy little girl grew up to be an intriguing young woman with intelligent brown eyes, auburn hair, and an engaging personality. The battle with her weight never seemed to be quite won, not that her many friends and clients ever noticed once they got talking to her – or had one of her marvelous confections.

Calliope Dancer never really liked her given name of Britney Alexandra and instead picked Calliope after a trip to the busy children's park down by the river. They played that awful circus music on the merry-go-round there, with the painted horses and an odd little man operating the ride on Sundays. He spun stories of steam pianos, traveling circuses, and Greek gods to Britney.

She gleefully explained them to her mother on the way home in the car. "It was just like he had been there and everything. I want you to call me Calliope now, like the muse Mr. Holroyd told me about. Mr. Holroyd said Calliope helped Homer write poetry. And she married the god of War, and she…"

"Okay Britney, that's enough now," her mother said, realizing just how long the drive home was becoming.

Her father exploded at dinner when she told him the stories as well, and then her new name. He forbade her ever going back again.

"How could you ever let her go off and talk to a stranger? My God, she was talking to the dog last week telling me he was telling her things about the neighborhood! Now this weird man at the park," he ranted, along with other similar warnings and prohibitions to her mother. Even so, Britney Alexandra became Calliope after that, no matter how loud her father yelled or how often her mother's sighed.

Her long suffering parents had first hoped she would take a normal interest in something, anything, but certainly not the odious concoctions derived from a crazy book sent by Calliope's mother's aunt, referred to as "that dingbat" by her father.

"It smells like boiled garbage with plastic floating in it," her father would rant. "And she is mixing it with all the sugar we have in the house too. I hope to God she is not eating it!"

When she sat around the house day after day doing nothing and becoming more useless had been bad enough. Now she was obsessed with cooking God knows what. It finally became too much and her parents banished her to the garage. She went happily with her book clutched to her chest, out with the boxes of smelly liquids and powders, and lots more room for her mixing and formulating.

She had been by now collecting her supplies around the neighborhood from both the natural environs and grocery stores and shops far off the beaten path. When she could not get her mother to take her to them, she took the city bus. Her father was certain it was just to aggravate him further when she told him of her outings and the people she met on her trips. She used her father's credit card to order ingredients from far away places, places with names like "Ahmed's Apothecary" or "English Alchemy."

"Enough is enough, even if she is finally taking some interest in something," father had said to mother while hustling Calliope out into the garage through the kitchen door with the gauzy white curtains over the window.

June had never understood her aunt Hermione for as long as she could remember. Hermione and Calliope always seemed to get along famously and would disappear together for days at a time with no accounting except a laconic, "we were exploring and auntie was explaining things," from Calliope. "Oh, don't fret so much, June, Calliope is a wonderful girl and we have a great time together," Hermione would say.

"I can't stand it!" Albert, Calliope's father, would rail to his wife. "She blows in from God knows where she is living anytime she just feels like it. Then she and our lazy daughter take off to God knows where, doing God knows what for days and days, and then they just wander back in! I can't stand it! I can't stand it!"

"Now Al," June would say with a blank frown. "Calliope is almost ten and Hermione always tells us when she is taking her out for a few days. I am sure everything will be all right. It always is. Besides, you said yourself you want Calliope out of the house more, don't you?"

"Stop, stop now she has you calling her that name! And no, I don't want her just traipsing off with that crazy aunt of yours. Your side of the family is all like this, all of them, weirdoes and kooks."

"Now Al, what about your cousin Herman and his experiments? He blew up the garage last summer with one of his 'alchemy science' experiments. The fire chief told you he was never allowed to visit us again, didn't he?"

"He is a second cousin on my mother's side. It isn't anything like a real relative anyway. And he was out there with Cal - ... BRITNEY BRITNEY ... now dammit she has me saying it. Besides, Britney probably helped cause it and did something she was not supposed to, so Herman got the blame."

"Now Al, she is our daughter and a lovely girl when she wants to be..."

And so the discussions in the Dancer house on the peaceful cul-de-sac went - not that Calliope paid much attention to them - even if most were about her.

Albert did do one thing for Calliope, although he didn't realize it. When he escaped the little house five days a week, he worked as a business consultant to numerous companies. He always told Calliope when she did something for somebody to always calculate the most she thought the client would pay and then add 20% to the bill.

"If you don't charge enough they will not keep paying you, and they will not listen to what you tell them," he would tell her. "I wish you would pay attention to me, and stop burying your nose in those crazy old books all your kooky relatives send you." She listened -- and read all the books carefully. She always remembered to charge plenty for her own unique brand of consulting, gleaned from all those kooky relatives and their books.

Her colorful home now hosted many odd visitors, demons and otherwise, who came to perch for a special treat and some much needed acceptance of those who must perform the nasties and unpleasantries of life for a living.

Cally got her share of scorn from the pedestrians of the regular world, but realized early that more interesting things happened behind the gates, fences, and walls erected to keep out the unimaginative rather than protect those behind them. The normal people had their rigid rules and regulations, but they were happy that way she figured. She did her part to take care not to step on their realities. She had learned the hard never to feed them her candy without proper supervision too.

She made the mistake as a child, carelessly giving a candy to a regular person once, some of great aunt's candy to one of her little friends. Not that there were many friends back then. The poor girl took it rather poorly, being shocked awake from the carefully regulated world of her parents, teachers, and community. Little Beth Anne sprinted home with her eyes wide open to tell mommy "she was simply full of shit" for having promulgated a bogus reality on her for all these years.

Fortunately uncle Herman happened to be visiting at the time. He had been through it with his and his wife's fourteen children, adopted and otherwise. It was just that he could not take in Beth Anne himself right now to get her ungrounded properly, so he went with Calliope to visit Beth Anne's hysterical and enraged parents. He took some of his own medicinal candy to put Beth Anne back into the groove her parents and peers had always assumed she had been in all along.

"She will never be the same you know, Calliope dear," he said on the way over. "This is one lesson even you will just have to follow. It's a hard one for people like us to learn, but many out there aren't really ready for your great aunt's brew, or anything you might concoct. She should've told. But, maybe this is better and it will stick with you now." He smiled at her way down from his towering height causing her to laugh, even if her father had ordered uncle to, "not make that horrible face in this house or around Calliope ever at all." Not that she seemed to mind it. Strange child.

***

"Oh dear, I seem to be out of cherry surprises," Calliope said, picking a lime crème out of the everyday drawer in the armoire for him instead, while she considered what to do about having no more cherry surprises at all. *I'll just have to mix up a batch as soon as possible if Tyrone has a problem I have to help him with.*

Her old friend slouched on the settee with his dark, pointy chin sunk upon his massive chest. Tyrone stared blankly at the rug Cally had purchased recently in Bucharest. The running patterns of colorful squares, lines, dogs, camels, and AK47s woven into the mid-1960s Caucuses carpet lying on the gray wooden planks in front of the cheerful loveseat did not seem to engage him. His long sigh was not a comment about Calliope's discovery that the cupboard held no more cherry surprises.

"Oh Ty, why so glum?" Calliope said, forgetting for a moment about the trauma of the candy shortage.

"Oh Calliope, I am really tired of my job."

"Why so?"

"No fun anymore."

Why do you think that is?"

"Just is."

8

"Does it make you sad?"

"Not fun anymore."

Calliope became concerned. Tyrone always talked up a storm, even for an employee of Nationwide Professional Services. These kinds of curt replies were not anything like him at all.

She selected a chocolate walnut coffee tropical cordial and handed it to the sad lump of glum on the couch. He would need it.

"Here, Tyrone, this will make you feel better. No, don't look at it that way, it's quite good and will cheer you up. I know it always does me."

He popped the morsel into his wide mouth and swallowed it whole.

"Oh Tyrone, you really should taste it. It is a very special candy and tastes absolutely divine."

"I am sorry Calliope. I am just not myself. This job dilemma is stretching my psyche to its limits, I dare say. The boss is being an absolute troll about it all, and the contract deadbeats I always am forced to deal with seem to be so much worse, really rather the worst ever in my many years in this profession."

Oh good, that's always the best truffle for this kind of thing, Calliope thought to herself as Tyrone droned on about how God awful things at work had become. *Now it sounds like the old Tyrone.*

When he had an account overdue the boss always called on him. He knew where the shirkers went to roost and how to persuade them to cough up the money. It was a dirty job, but somebody had to do it, and he was the best somebody at it around.

"I just have become weary of always having to visit Reno. Can you ever imagine what positively dreadful accommodations the biggest littlest city offers the jaded and fatigued bill collector, one who become un-enamored of the local so-called games of chance but however remains constrained to lodge there time over time whenever some miscreant bill dodger or other flees to its tired luster? Those mimes of the mentally deficient homing pigeon, returned to a filthy and broken coop in the eves of the decrepit manor house in which the proprietor is the most slovenly of innkeepers. Reno, where humans of a certain ilk are drawn to escape the obligations of Hell, fools they be, unaware it is but the firm's flypaper, trapping the lazy and unimaginative bill dodgers in its sticky embrace," he said in a much more animated version of his old self.

"Oh Tyrone, I did warn you not to gulp that confit in one snap. Now tell me what brings you to visit, not that you ever need a reason. You're always welcome in my home. Tell me about what's bothering you about your job that has brought you here," Calliope said, hearing Tyrone start to babble a bit from the candy.

"Like I said, I am off to Reno again to find a list of customers who owe us for services rendered on their behalf. It is the usual things my boss's customers contract for and then skip out on as soon as they think they can make away with it. Nationwide is like any other free market enterprise. It must have a steady cash flow or we are out of business. Heaven knows all the competitors are cued up salivating to abscond with the best of my company's business."

"I heard what you said about Reno. But it can't be that bad. You have been there many times."

"Well, with the Internet now, the dodgers are getting smarter and sharing ideas more than they have in times past. The damn Internet is a gift to the lazy and indolent and allows them to sit around on free Wi-Fi at Starbucks to figure new and better ways to duck out on their responsibilities."

"My, you sound just like another Far East client. He keeps after me to have dinner and help him find new ways to keep his people away from the online world. He's just adamant about it, but is always in a much better mood after a plain vanilla bon-bon or two. That way we can have a nice dinner and chin wag when I visit," Cally said with a smile. "But you still haven't told me exactly what brings you here tonight, Terrible Ty."

She always called him that. He liked it, truth be known. It made him smile, which was a frightening thing to behold. She never minded his cheerful leer that could freeze running water.

"Tell me why you are here, besides just having to go to Reno again. Is there more to it?"

"Yes, you are correct. It is more than just the job. Some of our best clientele are disappearing in unexplained ways. It is costing us money and my boss is furious about it.

"Very interesting. So it sounds like your boss is sending you to Reno to find out something."

"Only partially. Like I told you, many who are seeking to avoid their contracts run off there, so it is a happy hunting ground for me. But now it appears good customers are not even getting that far. Every now and then a client just vanishes, poof, gone, not hide nor hair left. I have two reasons to be there now."

"Then you're here to ask me if I know anything? This is the first I have heard of it, and I usually get that kind of news early."

"He has kept it very quiet so I am not surprised you are unaware of the issue. It has only begun to happen too, but his new big data enterprise software catches trends for this kind of thing quickly. It is always wise to keep up to date with good business tools just for this reason. I want to ask you to look into it for us if you have some time to spare. In fact, here is one of the incidents that I speak of," Tyrone said, taking out his smart phone and showing Calliope a story about the disappearance of a young woman in Portland.

"Well, Richard Branson has invited me to Davis to hear his World Economic Forum pitch for Virgin Galactic spaceship, but frankly, I have heard it before. Elon Musk and Jeff Bezos will be miffed if I go with Rich instead of taking time hear their own grand spaceship plans. I prefer to avoid that right now to keep everybody happy. No promises you understand. Besides, the trip to China last month wore me out. I could use a diversion from all the politics of both for a change."

"That is all I would dare to ask of you, Calliope. But he would certainly appreciate it and ... "

"Stop, Tyrone. We understand each other, and he already owes me. Like I said, a diversion if I get some time."

"Thank you so much for the treat and your company. I always enjoy our meetings. I hope you understand this was not just a mere business call for me?"

"I always look forward to your visits, Terrible Ty," she said with a smile.

Tyrone's laugh shook the walls as he stood up. "I must take my leave for Reno, much before I am ready," he said with a diabolical leer. "Godspeed, Ms. Dancer!"

"Very funny, TT," she said walking downstairs to the door with him. "No promises no matter how charming you try to be."

"Oh my, I must make an inventory," she said to herself returning to inspect the depleting candy drawers and considering what she would need for upcoming engagements.

Chapter 2

Joshua kept busy all morning hanging out in the Portland Saturday Market snatching newbies before other dealers of desire hooked them up. Circling pimps, hustlers, and sellers trading in temptation and indulgence drifted through the market stalls with him. They glided out to the edge of the market now and then, stopping in quiet pools with the baked skaters and want to be cools, lurking there for the rare new buyer coming to the market for the first time. Fresh blood drew them all, to unsheathe the hooks they kept under their tee shirt or mini-dress to snare the new lost soul. Occasionally Josh got to the mark first and made them a regular customer. It kept him in bud and paid the roommates often enough so they didn't kick him out.

"Hey Josh," the hard faced burgundy haired girl said to him. "How's it hanging?" Her dead eyes gave lie to the sweet smile she flashed. Everybody he hung with at the market did the same. It never registered with him now.

"Hey Reb. It's goin', sorta'. You?"

"I been doin' okay. Anything new?"

"I been thinking 'bout moving up to Seattle to take some tech classes and learn to code or something."

From their mouths to my ears, she thought. Before tina, weed, sex, swag or whatever other shit they used, stole, or sold, they had taken classes, or even managed to finish one once. Most were just about to start back again, had a plan, sorta, to move somewhere else and get back to normal, like mom and dad wanted. Friends, families and fools believed them once, or wanted to. Then they didn't believe anymore.

13

Keep saying it kid. Maybe it'll happen. Ha! Rebecca didn't give a fuck either, except to smile inwardly at his lame, predictable existence. It meant he was primed for her now. Big fish always eat the little fish, and so on. *Abandon hope, fucker.* "While you're getting packed up, Josh, I got some shit that has to move now," Rebecca said pushing her hips forward with her feet spread suggestively. She brushed her hand through her bright wine hair and put on half of a smile. Josh noticed. His mouth twitched.

"I'm about outta bud from Xavier. But he don't like changes. I don't know."

"Never mind, I don't have issues with him." *He sent me shithead so you can move more. Christ.*

"Well, I don't wanna rock the boat or nuthin', you know."

"I got chiva, honey. You can really score if you do it right. Do you think you can?" A troika of possible money, bud, and drug addled sex visions dragged him along.

"Yeah, I know what ta do," Joshua said tipping his chin up.

God, Xavier was right. What a fucking tool. "You just deliver to your customers. I can set you up. They order, you show up, drop it off, and drive off, and only carry a few hits in your mouth for them. That's how it's done, Josh. Do you understand? You get it? She said making sure he understood it.

"Yeah, I know how. Fuck. Don't keep sayin' it."

"You got a car don't ya?"

"Yeah, course I do."

By four, Rebecca had finally managed to get everything through his weed soaked head and passed him a number to call for a trial delivery. *Christ this loser will fuck it up in no time. He'll move a little cheap shit anyway.*

Finally she could head off to change and cruise the clubs for some fun after dealing with these nitwitted stoners all day. *They really take too much work* she thought on the way to her Mini on the roof of the Chinatown SmartPark garage.

She did her job well and had actually taken classes, with a marketing degree to prove it. Selling weed and building the network to do it hid under her innocent freckles in school. It paid for Brown University and the other good things she wanted and deserved. The drug network became the career after school. She put profitable use to the marketing knowledge by educating her business partners and increased the money dropping to her bottom line.

Rebecca rolled the electric blue BMW into her parking space in the Pearl District. She loved her repurposed industrial age real estate cum apartment house for the newly hip. The cold face under the glowing crimson hair warned anybody who might notice her heading through the lobby to look elsewhere. The relaxed, loose retro-hippy chick did not live here.

She ignored the bored lobby attendant and did not see the tiny curl of her lip as she sauntered by, answering her disposable burn phone and pulling back the forest green scissor gate on the gentrified freight elevator.

"Give me five, getting on an elevator," she said putting the phone away.

The phone rang later inside her stainless steel and black granite kitchen. She sat down on a chrome and red leather stool at the high stone bar across from the cavernous living room with the refinished wooden floor from the 1920's machine shop. The old pine beams above had once held flapping leather machine belts. Wood, leather, deco lamps, and retro throw rugs decorated the empty living space.

She sneered out over the darkening city through the meticulous steel latticed windows recycled from an unknown, unremembered brick building in the rust belt. The maid had not washed them. *I need to fire her ass.*

"Hi, Payaso, she answered the phone, sorry I had to cut off there... Yes, he's locked to deliver for K tonight... Right, he has a customer base to tap for the cheap shit and he's as dumb as shit. Keep him in weed and he'll be happy... Right, keep the good stuff till it cools off... I have the numbers for D and the plan to expand south that we talked about. *God, I already explained this to him. Why're they so thick?*

Xavier called himself El Payaso. You never knew who was listening and security tradecraft came easily or you did not last very long in business. Either the federals got you or the competition – or your friends. Rebecca had learned her own street smarts young, talking herself out of speeding tickets and twisting the unaware boys out of the arms of the other less savvy girls.

Rebecca had not recruited in a couple of years, but the feds had knocked over Xavier's network recently in a big public PR push to clean up in and around the Portland Saturday Market. The usual recruiters had gotten burned and had to go cool off for a while. Even the clown took a vacation to his estate on Maui for a few weeks. Rebecca had to pick up some of the slack and get new mules into the pipeline to put things back together. The cops did not know her as a street regular or a gang member. She always could make the possibles like Joshua easily and handle keeping the business going with the cheap red heroin and the new mules until things dropped back to normal. Then they could sell the better black tar again, dump the losers and bring the regular crew back.

The professional services contract Rebecca signed while in college had only taken 15% of gross earnings. She also had to provide detailed personal information on every person she turned to Nationwide Professional Services. In exchange she got special intelligence, training, and real time support to be able to spot any cop or law enforcement agent easily. She could see them without effort after the contract went into effect. Nationwide also gave her professional sales training for her unique products, network access to potential clients like Xavier, and legal representation if ever her spotting abilities let her down. The last bit served as a guarantee of sorts and she had never needed it.

Two or three times a year somebody would drop by to see if she wanted to buy any other services from Nationwide. Rebecca drove a hard bargain and her first and only service purchase had been very profitable up to now. She kept the payments up to date, never cheated on reporting her income, and steered new clients to Nationwide she knew would benefit her, and Nationwide too if it worked out that way. The Nationwide salespeople always went away disappointed. "Why do you bother," she told them. "I can see the pitch coming a mile away. I know what I am doing and will call you if I think I want something else from you."

She stepped out of the shower and into her black Temperley silk mini dress and purple Mark Schwartz open platform boots. She put her white gold and square cut emerald choker necklace and strode off to club to celebrate not having to hustle distribution deals to addled dopers for a few days. She was horny, sans underwear, and wanted to get laid tonight.

The Electron had a long line when Rebecca arrived and turned the Mini over to the valet. She strutted over to the roped off section for VIPs scowling at the blond man guarding the entrance.

"Good evening, Ms. Carlile," he said nodding to her.

"Hello," she said looking down at her dress and boots while he unhooked the entrance rope and held it back for her. She sauntered proudly down the roped VIP lane and into the loud club, ignoring the looks from the everyday patron line and the attendant holding the rope for her.

None of the young hipsters or the hookers looking for them and their money appealed to her when she swaggered into the commotion inside The Electron. She ordered her first drink and surveyed the crowd, dismayed with the prospects packing the room. *The*

*women dress like the skanks at the Market, ick. They should
pay me to lick me. I don't want a girl tonight anyway. But
God, the pale pussy excuses for men. Skanks all of them.* She
sat down sour faced to finish her second drink and then
tramped back outside the way she had come in.

The line at the entrance was even longer than
when she arrived, and the music coming out the door
louder. The valets were off getting cars and she did not
want to wait. She headed in the direction of younger
meat markets a few blocks over, turning down the
broken sidewalk in front of the club to take a shortcut
through an alley into the empty commuter parking lot
behind The Electron. From there, she could cross over
to another street with the club she was lusting after.

Rebecca enjoyed the sensuous slip of the silk on
her naked body and reveled in the building lust while
she swayed across the dark asphalt of the parking lot in
her sexy heels. The weak streetlight behind the line of
businesses next to The Electron cast a flickering shadow
of her catlike walk as she thought about where she'd
pursue her night's pleasure. *I feel like breaking in some
young cock tonight. Yum.*

Rebecca ignored the scrabble from the shadows
behind her next to the back of the buildings adjoining
The Electron, sounds made by shadows meant for low
level types other than her. The snap of her neck and
crushing of the top of her skull only made a brief
crunching sound. No scream accompanied them, only
the sharp exhale of her final breath. She did not feel
when her limp body hit the ground or when the
slippery spikes pierced it. No one noticed the quiet
commotion behind the dumpsters next to the broken,
oil-stained asphalt of the Park R'U lot.

The smiling young woman on the white Giant
bicycle picked up the boots and necklace the next
morning underneath the Old Camp Casino billboard on
her way to work. She passed the scattered dumpsters
every morning and sometimes found something
interesting thrown out from the clubs and bars the night
before. The tall slinky boots were sticky and gross. She

would not even touch the slimy puddle with the shimmering blue cloth crumpled in it. Maybe she could clean up the funky footwear and the retro costume jewelry to use for her cosplay costume next month at the comic-con. It was worth a try.

Mike Macartney

Chapter 3
Central Nevada 1888

Falling ... Heat ... Impact ... Silence. The last bits of the machine spent.

He became expendable when the energy ran out. Only a few remaining would continue to race quietly through the soft blackness for the next island. The best that could be done now meant sending him off in the direction of a nearby star with planets.

He would have to wait for the healing to progress. He would bury shards of machine deep in the gritty earth where the spreading toe of the rocky fan flowed out from the dry mountains. The sand and gravel would creep a little more over it each time the waters came.

He would need biological chemicals and energy for his body and the few remaining machines from the wreckage to survive now. With them he could. He was made that way. He once served to guard an ambassador. Now he served himself and his own survival. He could even change to become an ambassador if his survival succeeded and the intelligent life in this place could recognize such an emissary.

He existed as layers upon layers of contingencies, potentials, and possibilities, like the striped mountain stone around him. He could with time, energy, and chemicals twist and fold his layers to form new selves. He could become like any one of the others he traveled with when a contingency became a necessity. His architecture would be severely strained now just to heal. Better to remain the protector form he was built as until he understood more.

The fleeing remnants of the ship might keep the others alive until the next world, or not. They might come back for him someday, or not. He became a mission himself and started the task of survival. His mind flowed in two smooth streams. One mulled his immediate environment and its potentials, while the other assembled internal resources to build alternative plans for any contact with whatever intelligence might live in this place. He might never encounter any intelligence at all and would exist only as a protector here for all the foreseeable future. Neither future nor past held any relevance for him. His makers made him able to endure the centuries of travel demanded by the void. Unlike theirs his mind would remain sane through the interminable quiet aloneness of the voyage. With energy and chemical supplies he could wait indefinitely. Pursuing one particular future in one particular form was pointless. Infinite and unknown possibilities extended in all time and directions from his spontaneous living self. That's how he was made.

His chemical and light sensors allowed him to locate small life forms near his broken body. They came to take his chemicals, he took theirs. He dissolved them in a rapid digestive solvent to separate the building blocks and begin the process of repairing and reshaping himself. The nearby star provided enough energy to keep his chemical processes going. The oxygen and other gasses in the atmosphere were plentiful and helped speed the processes. It powered the few fragments of equipment he had taken to assist in his healing and reconfiguring if he encountered a new place where it might be possible.

The ship had traveled far from its makers, visiting places and beings that had contributed their own technology to it and its crew. He was no longer the creature that had been sent out and had more ways to survive and morph than the makers had dreamed of. It was how he was made.

He watched one creature in particular on his new world. It moved on eight appendages and injected digestive solvents into other inhabitants around it in order to consume their chemicals. It had multiple sensors on its body and its hydraulic actuation inside a tough exoskeleton made it very powerful. It could move rapidly. He decided it would be a strong protector form in his new world. He began the long repair and reformation of his body to this creature's physical model. Its form could house his brain deep inside and would have the strength and sensing he would need here to meet whatever contingencies this planet demanded.

***

He had observed the most intelligent life forms carefully for a long time. The lone individual coming up the trail would be his first direct encounter with them.

It made obvious communication sounds towards him. He began to imitate it and to learn.

Mike Macartney

Chapter 4
Paris, France May 2014

François Hollande could not keep his lecherous hands to himself now that his girlfriend had dumped him. It was not any different from the times when she was still around.

"But, Calliope, come by tonight after the dinner."

"I am sorry Frankie honey, you know I only came to pick up some wonderful Paris butter crème from Michel. Nobody makes it like he does," Cally said, her mouth watering just thinking about the butter crème she could now get directly to take home from France.

She could not pass up a dinner at the Palais de l'Élysée, even if Nick Sarkozy was no longer President. He had the most crafty and interesting mind, and Calliope always enjoyed the free ranging meals with his navigating through the tangled web of politics and celebrity swirling around him. He did most certainly object to being called Nick, though. He would shout at her when she called him that, but with a twinkle in his dark eyes too. François lacked Nick's imagination and panache.

Oh well, the food is quite good and the chocolate divine, she thought to herself. *Great Aunt Hermione always liked French chocolate best and thought it made the candy more effective for seeing the world better and influencing others. It seems to and I must try some new things with it.*

"I can arrange to have Carlotta join us if you like, dear," François said interrupting her reverie while leering at her from his chair. "She is one of Silvio

Burlusconi's favorites. You know how he can pick them, even if he is not Italian Prime Minister anymore."

"No thank you, Frankie, I have a headache tonight," Cally said. He hated being called Frankie and made a stern face at her before the tight little smile popped back.

The supper repartee flowed along without significant international incident and Calliope managed to enjoy the food and avoid the bedroom entanglements. Finally, after all his attempts failed François had his Groupe de Sécurité de la Présidence de la République agents escort Calliope to the door where the Citroen hybrid limo France provided waited for her.

"Do come again soon. You know we have much more to discuss. This surprise supper was too short to discuss your ideas for dealing with the little troll. It seems you know him quite well. And there is still Carlotta too," François said, waving as she climbed in. "The chauffer will take you wherever you like – hopefully back here later this evening."

"Thank you so much Frankie, but I really don't need the car. We will get together again soon I am sure," she said, closing the window and waving the driver to start. Her host's little smile did not cover the pout and irritation as well as it usually did this time. The French secret service agents tried not to smile at all.

Cally asked the driver to drop her off in the Sixth Arrondissement where she got out to take a stroll there around the Saint-Germain-des-Prés in the pleasant evening.

The hand slipping into her pocket was not there to excite her. She clamped hers on a tiny wrist attached to a startled little girl and held her before she could bolt. "Now dear, that is not polite at all," she said to the sullen child as her father sidled up to them. At least he might be her father in a more genteel time and place, just a fellow pickpocket here.

The police had been targeting the gypsies around the fancy shops. The mayor was just aghast that the Roma were being profiled – in liberal and tolerant

Paris, too. These two had gotten past the mayor somehow.

"Oh, is you Miss Calliope." the dark older man said recognizing her. "Sorry bother you. "Tsura, is friend okay. Go now."

The girl walked down the sidewalk to covertly scope out the German tourist group getting off a bus.

"She is young. Why you here, Miss Calliope?"

"I needed to restock some of my special candy ingredients that only Paris can do right, and could not pass up a very good dinner offer from a friend. This is a wonderful place to walk off the butter before I head home. Would you like one of these Swiss chocolate coconut trifles, Yanko? They are my own recipes."

Cally recalled her late night conversation with Tyrone and decided this might be a good a time to poke into what he had told her. Yanko knew as much as anyone about the less legal side of life in Paris. She had promised Tyrone and had been lazy about getting to it.

"Ah, Miss Calliope always you have candy. Thanks you," he said taking the morsel she offered blithely.

That one will make him talk a little more.

"Yanko, maybe you can tell me something? Have there been any unusual disappearances here lately? Especially disappearances of people outside of the law if you understand me," she said recalling Tyrone's story about a client who disappeared in Portland.

"What you mean unusual?"

"It's hard to describe. Have any of your more successful – profitable – friends or acquaintances just up and disappeared? Not the usual ways, like where they crossed the wrong person or did business in the wrong place?"

"Hum, that Roma business," he said looking hard at her through narrowed eyes. "You good friend though. Not tell wrong people. Maybe I tell something."

"Thank you, Yanko. My lips are sealed," she said, putting her fingertips to her mouth. "Let's walk and talk, shall we."

"Miss Calliope, let us say he was name Victor. He very young to have such big influence in Monaco with all the others there. Many Russia like him there, you understand?"

"Da," Calliope said without moving her mouth. She looked down the sidewalk as she listened to Yanko's sotto voice.

"Victor come to Paris to meet Le Milieu, you know Corsicans from the south. It one year, maybe, summer. The Corsicans hate him like all Russian Bratva. Take too much good business in south and not be afraid of them, yes?"

"Yes."

"But, you know Corsicans afraid Victor and Russians, but need their money and have to work with them. Then, whoosh, he gone. Come to meet and then no more."

"Hum."

"Yes, nobody know and nobody never find him. Corsicans tell everybody not do it so make sure Russians know they not do it because very afraid Russians. Russians finally believe them, but take more business from Corsicans anyway. It good for Russians Corsicans old and afraid, so they take more. Like wolves, you understand?"

"Yes."

"Roma smart to stay out of it. We have own business. All I say. Roma business like I say. Is what you want to know?"

"Yes, Yanko. You are a good friend. Here is a strawberry daiquiri white chocolate for you and also one for Tsura. Go to her. She looks like she needs you to come."

Calliope had noticed Tsura getting nervous. The Germans were getting away while Yanko talked too much. She kept furtively looking over at Calliope and

28

Yanko coming up the sidewalk. She wanted to get after her quarry.

The candy would make them cheerful and relaxed for the rest of their night shift preying on the tourists in the district. They would remember little of the meeting with Calliope. *Better safe than sorry with the Russians involved.*

Cally enjoyed Paris immensely and would have preferred a longer, more leisurely stay. There were other people to see, more good food to consume, and French wine to drink. It had been a long day. *I really don't feel like going all the way home tonight, but my own bed does sound inviting.*

There was always her invitation to return to the Palace and join François and Carlotta. She had promised to spend more time with him since his election to talk about services she could provide, but he always was a bit of a stiff and way too grabby now that Valerie had moved on. Going to the Palace was too difficult at least tonight. She had sent the car back with regrets in any case.

Cally finally decided to walk over to the Buddha Bar to see about a suite for the night. It was always one of her favorite spots in Paris. They had the best exotic décor, and she loved their red walls. Feeling that it would be a bother to talk to the front desk and realizing she could run into somebody she knew in the lobby, she walked up to look in upper level windows until she found an empty suite. At 2:13 AM she figured the odds were, even in Paris, nobody would be checking into the hotel.

The king sized bed looked very inviting, so she let herself in. After taking a quick look at the luxurious décor and cloudlike bed she slid under the padded quilting and fell right to sleep without going downstairs to register, after hanging the "Ne pas déranger" sign on the hallway door handle to ensure there would be no entry by late arrivals or early maids.

Snuggling down into the bed Calliope drifted off with memories of when she first learned how she could just walk wherever she wish to. Her parents never knew that some of her jaunts with Great Aunt Hermione were much farther from the little California suburban ranch house than they ever imagined. Her first trip to India when she was twelve ushered in the most pleasant dreams.

After a nine o'clock shower Calliope felt awake enough to go downstairs and have well-deserved delicious breakfast at the hotel. *Why be in France if not to eat croissant and other fresh pastries and bread?* She left a plain candy treat for the maids next to a note and went down to the front desk on her way outside to choose the best restaurant to have her breakfast.

"What!" the clerk at the desk shouted when she told him about the room in her accented French that he pretended not to understand at first. "You slept in a room and did not pay. How did you get in, you thief? You Americans think you can do anything, anything at all! I will have the gendarme here in a moment. Then we shall see how you like it."

"My, no candy for you," Cally said smiling. "I will be having breakfast in the hotel if you need me."

The garden courtyard in the Le Veraymonde hotel restaurant had an open table and Cally didn't have to wait to be seated. She had just ordered a Belgian waffle and was about to relax with her first cup of wonderful dark French coffee when a voice interrupted her first sip.

"Madame, I have the gendarme," the desk clerk said, bouncing up to her table with a gleeful smile.

"Oh, so you do. And you are, Sir?" she said, turning to the middle aged man wearing a crisp **Police Nationale** uniform with the rank of major on his shoulders.

"Excuse me, Madame, but did you break into this hotel during the night and sleep in a room without paying? I am told you did so," he said to Calliope.

"Why yes, I did use the room, but I did not break anything. It was very late and I was tired. I certainly planned to pay this morning."

"Yes, see, I told you it was so," the clerk shrieked. "A thief. She stole a room and admits it now."

"Oh. Then you will pay? And maybe there was nobody at the desk when you came in?" the major said looking, for a way to get out of the developing scene at the elegant restaurant.

"No, no. Arrest her. She broke in. She destroyed hotel property and did not pay."

The major wanted to end this. People at other tables were turning to watch.

"Madame, did you break in to the hotel, the room?"

"Oh no, I just opened the door. I would never break it."

"And you, sir," the major said, turning to the clerk and interrupting his building outburst. "What was broken?"

"Why, she broke in. All the rooms are locked electronically for the protection of our guests. She had to break the door to get in."

"Excuse me Major, my breakfast is here. Would you please call this number to check about me," she said handing him a card. She gave the smug clerk her Visa Black card. "Take this for the room, sir."

Cally turned to the huge golden brown waffle with fruit, whipped cream, and chocolate sauce the irritated waiter finally was able to put before her.

The hotel clerk gaped at the card then sneered at being dismissed in such a manner. "Now wait," he started.

"Now you will charge her for any room cost and damage, and I will make a call," the major said with a steely look at the clerk after looking at the card Calliope had handed him from the **Groupe de Sécurité de la Présidence de la République**, the one from the Palais de l'Élysée the night before.

The major handed Calliope her credit card once the officious clerk returned with the receipt. "Everything is taken care of, Madame."

31

"Oh, thank you. I am so sorry about the commotion."

"It is taken care of. If there is anything else I can do for you please let me know."

I believe there might be, Major. And I am sorry, what is your name?"

"Henri DuMonde, Madame."

"Well, Major DuMonde, please call me Calliope. Do have one of these chocolate walnut coffee tropical cordials. It is quite good. I would very much like to ask you about a Russian gentleman that may have disappeared recently."

The major looked at the candy and then thought of the card he had handed back to Calliope before eating it.

"This is quite good," he said honestly. "Something from the best Paris chocolatier I am sure."

"It has the very best French chocolate. I am glad you like it."

Henri had coffee and a chocolate croissant while he waited to get permission from his commander to speak with Calliope. Major DuMonde told Calliope all about his love life, and his plans for advancing into the management side of the force, the Corps de Commandement et d'enCadrement, in the meantime. He had an uncle on that side of the force and would soon be taking the civil service tests for the rank of lieutenant, or inspector, as Calliope might call it. He fully expected to pass with his uncle's help. He hoped Cally might offer to help smooth the promotion with her obvious high level contacts. Maybe she could help him go even farther.

"Wouldn't it be quite grand to join the secret service, if you might be able to assist me. I had never dreamed of it before," he said wide eyed at his possible good fortune at meeting such a woman this morning.

A quick stepping superintendent arrived, smiling at Calliope as she sipped her coffee. Major DuMonde snapped to attention and stood so abruptly their cups tinkled in their saucers. The superintendent assumed his air of command with the major and returned the salute. "Thank you, Major. This is a divisional matter now," he said turning back to the mysterious woman with connections to the President he had been sent to assist.

"Madame, may I be of service? I understand you have an interest in a minor event here in Paris."

"It is very nice to meet you …"

"Divisional Superintendent Gordinier, Madame. And you are?"

"Calliope Dancer, Superintendent. As I said I am very pleased to meet you, Superintendent Gordiner. I do hope I have not inconvenienced you. I did not intend to do that with my question to Major DuMonde."

The major still stood next to them with a good bit of pique showing. He had been cut completely out of the exchange.

"Oh, and, I would like to thank you and the excellent officer here," she said looking back to Henri with a big smile. "He has been a tremendous help to me and I know you sent one of your best police officers over when you did."

Major DuMonde beamed at the compliment, but did not have a chance to even thank the good Madame Dancer before the Superintendent gave him a brusque nod to move along quickly back to his duties elsewhere.

"Now Madame Dancer, what was it you would like to know?" the Superintendent asked Calliope.

"Well, Superintendent, I have been asked by a good friend, who is also a client to look into the disappearance of some rather dangerous criminals he is investigating. I am not a police officer myself, but he knew I have good friends here in France who are. He asked me if I might ask around to help his investigation. I have heard there have been some Russian gangsters who have gone missing lately. Would you be able to tell me anything about it? I would very much appreciate it if you could."

The Police Nationale knew about Victor's disappearance. After some trepidation about disclosing official information the Superintendent begrudgingly decided to comply with the direction explicitly given by his immediate superiors, who had themselves called the Groupe de Sécurité de la Présidence de la République to check on this crazy American. He scowled, remembering hanging up with the last call from his boss realizing he would have to "assist Madame Dancer in any way she desires."

He told her several others like Victor had also vanished in odd circumstances in the sewers under Paris. The bodies appeared to have been dissolved there with an unknown chemical agent, not the crude barrels of drain cleaner the Mexican drug gangs she might have heard of used for disposing of their victims. The Superintendent offered to take Calliope to visit one of the areas where one of the disposals appeared to have been carried out " ... as long as you do not object to water and some bad odors." He really did not expect her to come and actually had never made a visit himself – he did not care for water and bad odors at all. That was what underlings were for. However, politics being what they are, he figured it might look good to make a visit with a politically connected foreigner. It might also deflect some of the pressure he was under to make headway in the case. It involved the dangerous Russian Mafia and possibly other organized crime groups, and he suspected his boss dumped everything in his lap to deal with this just in case it might look bad for him.

**

The little locomotives drawing carts and the boats carrying visitors through the famous sewers had been retired long ago, but the sewers remained. The National Police could enter wherever they wished of course, and Superintendent Gordinier made a series of calls while his driver took them to a sewer entrance at the edge of Paris in the 18ᵗʰ Arrondissement.

"Madame Dancer, I have arranged a special visit. The best investigators from the National Forensic Science Institute are there now. I have instructed them to cooperate with your inquiries," he said with an irritated look after a heated exchange on his cell phone. He did not mention to Calliope that the Director General's office had told both he and the Institut national de police scientifique (INPS) to arrange the visit if it would help to move this case forward in most certain terms.

They entered the sewer to be bathed in a fecund humidity reeking of the biological remains of the famous cuisine of the great city. A low-slung natural gas powered cart driven by a bored sewer worker drove them deep into the underground maze to where the police laboratory technicians worked.

"Madame Dancer, may I introduce Doctor Fignon. He is in charge of the technical investigation," Gordinier said, walking up to a huge man in a jumpsuit staring down at a mess on the floor. The technicians worked in a huge chamber where three other smaller channels dumped from the walls into it and emptied into the large tunnel that Calliope's party had come through.

The towering doctor's irritation flared at this intrusion into his work by an arrogant political climber with some snoopy foreigner in an evening dress in tow.

"I am sorry Superintendent, we are very busy here. I do not need these distractions at all if I am to solve this. Why are you here bothering us?" he began abruptly, glaring down at the Superintendent and ignoring Calliope completely.

"Now just a moment, Doctor, my direction comes directly from ... " Superintendent Gordinier started to say.

"I don't give a fuck if your orders come from God on high in triplicate delivered by fucking angels," thundered the great bear leaning over them. "My job is unwinding this mess your people have thrown on us because you would rather lead a parade of fucking tourists down here to interfere than do any work yourselves."

"Doctor Fignon, I have heard that your lecture at the Santa Fe Institute on the light polarizing compounds produced by cephalopods was very well received last summer," Calliope said.

"What ... say you?" the flummoxed doctor said, turning to look at Calliope for the first time.

"Yes, Murray enjoyed it immensely."

"Who? Are you talking about ... "

"Oh yes, Professor Gell-Mann and I had a wonderful lunch when he visited Stanford for a complexity conference. The pattern generation behavior of the cephalopod cells and the related chemicals they employ seem to very much fall into the realm of complexity theory, he believes. He is now absorbed with how biological chameleon defense mechanisms activate from signals from their complex eyes, to their brains, then to the cells on their bodies. It appears to be an instantaneous process with very efficient or very little pattern processing along the nerve pathways."

"Well, how fascinating. Paul here never brings anybody with a brain down here," Doctor Fignon said, nodding in the direction of the fuming politico. "If you would care to fill me in on what Professor Gell-Mann said about chemistry and complexity, I should be delighted to enlighten you about some of the interesting things we are finding here."

He led Cally over to a pile of cloth and started telling her what they had found there.

"As you may have been told, we have had several discoveries down here of what appear to be human remains. The Russian gangster Mikhail "Misha" Genkin vanished, and we found his ID in one of these little deposits," he said nodding down at the stiff clothes strewn at their feet.

"The disposal chemical used has unique properties. Only some the clothing and synthetic materials survive and are coated with a confusing mix of biochemical residues when we find them. We are only able to tie these sites to people because of the bits of identification and personal items we find in them. Even the DNA in the residue is broken by the unknown agents and is useless for identifying the victims directly."

"How did you come to find them?" Calliope asked, enjoying the discussion that reminded her of her science and chemistry professors.

"It started with the disappearance of some of the massive wooden balls used to clean the sewers. The sanitation workers found them torn apart when they went looking for them. You can see one over there," he said pointing to scattered chunks of wood along the wall of the concrete chamber they stood in.

"The personal effects and chemicals turned up near the shattered cleaning balls. The sewer managers called in the police and they immediately suspected some kind of terrorist cell had come to take over the sewers. That's what police do in France," the Doctor said smiling sweetly at the sour Superintendent.

"So you're finding other remains of Russian Bratva?"

"No no, Misha had his own special fame to lend to the police theories of dark and sinister goings on under the streets. Most of the others we have found are just low level thugs and street crawlers."

"How many do you think there are?"

"It is hard to say. We have found four, but they are in remote parts of the sewer system and may have been there for some time, a few years at least. This one was found just a few days ago when they missed another cleaner. It is still damp, as you can see, not too old. Maybe we can trace the identification to a missing person and a time they disappeared. This may be a break since the others were older victims and very hard figure out after all that time. These people disappear and nobody much notices or reports it, and they are quickly forgotten. Misha was different, since we have been watching him for some time and when he vanished we knew about it."

"Now Madame Dancer, please do tell me about what Professor Gell-Mann had to say about chemistry," Doctor Fignon said looking down at Calliope with a smile.

"Oh, it's Calliope. Please call me Calliope, Doctor."

"Certainly, and you should call me Claude."

"Do join me for lunch and we can continue this conversation in a more appropriate place."

"Now wait, what about the investigation?" the forgotten Superintendent said to them as they walked over to the bored sewer worker and his cart.

"Oh Superintendent, I have what I need. You can carry on," Doctor Fignon said over his shoulder as he climbed into the cart.

Cally handed the driver a candy which considerably brightened him up, and they drove off leaving the politician in the sewer.

"Would you like one of these delightful little morsels?" Calliope asked Claude when they escaped the stifling sewer.

"Yes, indeed. France has the very best chocolates, wouldn't you agree?"

"Yes, I always come here for the chocolates as well as for the makings. These are my own recipes."

"Really, and you make chocolate too, delightful," he said taking a bite.

Chapter 5

Paris, France May 2014

Calliope thought she really must have to return home after lunch with Doctor Fignon while on the way to the restaurant with him.

It's a long walk on an empty stomach. I wish brought a bicycle. It's France after all. I always forget that. Damn this dress. It wouldn't have worked anyway. Why did I stay so long? Tyrone really owes me now.

Claude took her to his favorite bistro near the laboratory office where all the scientists and technicians came for food, coffee, and arguing. Loud theories, ideas, and opinions filled the air. Music, loungers, and tourists did not play well with the random outbursts from what first appeared to be quiet conversations between unfashionably dressed people of varying ages and upkeep. The waiters were accustomed to the sudden bouts of yelling and arm waving and paid no mind.

Calliope and Claude soon attracted several other scientists who all wanted to hear about what scientific conferences Calliope had attended America, and how Doctor Fignon was handling all the attention to his work on the bodies in the sewer. As a scientist, not a civil servant, he relished the technical exchange. He only referred to his onerous management duties and the blocked-headed official minders when he needed to explain why he did not have the time to do his real work.

Calliope handed out candy and made many new friends who all invited her back. They made her promise to come to all their next seminars.

It was like being back in college again, when Calliope discovered organic chemistry and what she could do with it and her candy to help her understand other people's complex problems. She had found the smarter and more connected the people were the more interesting were the issues they struggled with, and how willing they were to have the insight her concoctions provided. Soon she met heads of university departments, university presidents, and then the political and money people they connected with. It was the beginning of a very different kind of career for Calliope.

***

"Hallo Calliope!" the albatross said floating up beside her. "What are you doing this far from home? I thought it was Jasmine Smyth lost on the wrong side of the pond come to see Jimmy The Shyster about the disappearing of her worthless old man. He went down to the bodega to score some smokes after layin' inta her bout nuthin' 'cept her lousy cookin', 'n how she never bothered to get herself tricked out for him no more. With her it was always the johns, ' 'cause they pay the freight on this two-bit fleabag you call a home.' She'd yell n' he'd slam the door to, 'go get some smokes n' whatever else I feel like tonight.' She'd cry into her frilly hanky 'bout how it weren't that way when they first met 'n go hit the sauce at Frankie's place and sidle upta guys like me cause we, 'look like nice guys. ' That's ... "

"Stop, Clarence, you have been reading those old books in the dumpster again. And yes, I am heading home from a visit to Paris," Cally said, not breaking her pedaling.

She decided on a bicycle after all. She went into the Velo & Oxygen and got herself a brand new Gitane Vélos de Course with electric shifters. She could not buy a Gitane in the United States any more and thought it would be the perfect bike to bring back with her. She needed clothes and bike shoes too, and a pack to put her dress and purse in. The vintage yellow, red, and black Système U-Gitane jersey was nice to change into after wearing a stifling evening gown for almost two days. Sprinting across the Atlantic on her new Gallic racing machine while imagining a descent down the Alps in Le Tour was a delightful way to head home from Paris.

"Why did you high tail it outta Frisco for some R&R across the pond? Food, frolic, and frappé beside the sidewalks, some cheap brandy in the walk down dives on the backside of the city tourists never find on the maps?" the albatross said, taking a slow flap and tweaking a wingtip to match her slower pace.

"Oh yes, the food is always quite good in Paris," she said fondly remembering the chocolate soufflé at the Palace. "I went for dinner, chocolate, and a few business development things, but it turned into work. It was too much to and fro across the city and then under it too. I will finally sleep in my own bed tonight, having replenished the larder with much it lacked. I just wish Marcel, my snoopy chocolatier, would not always try to wheedle recipes from me for his own use. Oh well, it's his charm I guess."

"Ahh, so some sad sack put the touch on you to help him out. You dames are always too soft and fall for those big sad brown eyes. They see you comin' and stick out a foot, and BAM! you fall for 'em like a ton of bricks off a bad ladder on a rainy day."

"Jesus H., Clarence, this is worse than when you were reading the Harry Potter books! Yes, work of sorts. Tyrone, you know him, the talkative one, not as bad as you today though, nothing could be that bad, asked me to look into some strange goings on with some of his bosses' customers. I like him, Tyrone that is, not your *noir* imitation. His boss is a suit, though, but regardless I will look into it to see if something entertaining results. Now you have me babbling, sheesh."

"Don't be trusting the big boss man, it's always dough with him, 'n he always buys suits off the rack to save a buffalo. He can pinch 'n make into a dime when he wants to. He'd jack up his dyin' grandmother to get a nickel, so you better watch over yer own shoulder, or he'll be pattin' yer back while he lifts your purse with the other one."

"Ha, you got it. I suppose I should drop by his office and see what he really wants. I'll tell him I will poke around as a favor to a friend, no charge. Free always gladdens *his cheapness* so he might have something to say if it costs him nothing and helps his *business*. Now, have you heard anything happening I should know about? Something out of the ordinary, at least ordinary for you, whatever that is."

"Hum, since you's brought the boss up, I been hearin' the drums 'bout Chinatown from the boys way over east of here, if you get my drift."

"Chinatown? Huh, I don't follow you. What are you trying to say?"

"I am hearing some bad things, things about a war brewing. It isn't very detailed, just some gossip here and there about Chinese involvement of some kind. That's all I know, some vague rumors," Clarence said dropping his noir speak.

"You mean a war with Appleyard and some Chinese group? I don't get it."

Clarence screeched a laugh. "It's all I c'n say. I seez the Danish mob down there snatchin' up mackerel right under our noses. Better drop by and put the touch on 'em for a little tax on their scam." He flicked a wingtip in parting. "Seez you 'round, Calliope."

"Not if I seez you first, because my ears can't stand it. Stay away from those books!" she said waving and spinning up her pedaling to get back on top of the gear. *A war with Chinese and Appleyard, WTF? Eesh, I really must get home now.*

***

Home in San Francisco came with the evening star, a spin down Van Ness to California, and straight on till her very own rooftop in Pacific Heights. She left the bike upstairs, threw off her shoes, and ran down to grab three specials from the armoire plus a bottle of bold California Shiraz with a very large glass from the dining room. She proceeded to the deep claw foot tub. Her very own bath preparations stood in cheerful lines of vibrant glass decanters on honey yellow sandstone beside it. Home is where the candy, wine, bubble bath, hot water, and clean sheets are.

The gray fog of the Pacific marine layer had begun to burn off, permitting splotches of weak blue here and there when Calliope came back to consciousness in her own bed late the next morning. It took her forty-five minutes to get out of bed, into a sweat suit, and downstairs to corn flakes, coffee, toast, strawberry preserves, and her phone to flip through her waiting email.

Thank God I don't give my email to very many people, she thought, scrolling through the 483 messages that had come up like bad mushrooms since she had left for Paris. *When was it, two days, three? No, I don't even remember now, what's today? Only Wednesday. It feels like a week. Oh shit, just who I need:*

What are you doing?

From The Desk Of The CEO
To: Calliope A. Dancer

Ms. Dancer.
We have been informed that you have undertaken some delicate inquires on our behalf. Please be advised your actions have not been authorized nor approved by us, and we are not liable for any expenses or obligations you might incur as a result of your own independent actions.

We can be reached at the above email if you wish to discuss this matter. You may also contact our administrative assistant should you wish to come in to see us in person. As you are aware, we are very busy and there are many demands upon our time. Therefore, any face-to-face meeting must be arranged in advance and will be of necessity short and to the point. Time is money.

Regards,

H. W. Appleyard, President and CEO
Nationwide Professional Services

"When I was young I thought that money was the most important thing in life; now that I am old I know that it is."
Oscar Wilde

Oh lord, he never changes. "We are very busy and will not pay for anything." No wonder people think you're such a fucking pill. Yeah, I'll call for an appointment. Oh puhleese, Henry, get over yourself. I am summoned? Really? This will cost you extra, my greedy little weasel. My services aren't cheap. Cheapskate."

She zipped farther into the muck of her inbox before finally starting wholesale filing of unimportant messages into her *fuck you* folder and deleting others – she could no longer face all of them. Calliope unplugged her phone from the charger and went to a more comfortable chair to call Tyrone to find out what he had been hearing while she was gone. *I really, really have to get somebody to deal with this mess, or dump this email and use one of my others more. Too many people know this one.*

When Tyrone picked up her call she told him what she learned on her trip. He seemed irritated though. He had not heard about Misha before now. She told him she'd look further, but said nothing about her email from Henry Appleyard. *He probably reported what I was doing anyway.*

44

She phoned a couple more clients putting out some feelers for new consulting business and providing status updates to clients on the few cases she had at present before she sat down at the laptop to write invoices and pay bills.

The late afternoon and evening were much more fun. Calliope stopped work early to enjoy cooking up batches of candy to replenish her depleted stores.

As she tempered a batch of Marcel's chocolate she opened a jar of butter crème and some of the other fillings he sold to her, including some wonderful extracts of nuts.

It took time to make more lime extract and the wild cherry flavors and extracts. Cooking the other cherry additives was tricky. They could easily become toxic if done wrong or the constituents were collected at the wrong time of the year.

Many kinds of fruit and nut extracts were already well represented in her candy pantry that she could use tonight along with the scores of more exotic powders and liquids there.

Besides making her more traditional sweet confections, she wanted to try adapting one of her great aunt's potions using Rasayana formulations from a book a fellow candy experimenter from Lahore had sent her. *They always have the most wonderful fruit squashes.*

It turned out most vile and ended up going down the sink. As midnight approached Calliope stopped for the day to settle down with more Shiraz and a DVD of *The Maltese Falcon*. First came the annoying chore of responding to Henry Appleyard about the meeting she had been putting off all day. That done she watched the movie until she fell asleep in her big leather easy chair.

In her dreams the old movie about hidden secrets from deep in the past, unknown bosses pulling strings, decoys, criminals, and tough guys assailed her subconscious concerns about Tyrone's problem, all tangled up with her visit to the old country with its storied   sewer   hiding   its   own   mysteries   deep underground.

Chapter 6

Reno, Nevada June 2014

Tyrone perched on a high stool at a tall table in the food court at Circus Circus, idly watching the young couples and families drift around aimlessly on another Friday night in Reno. His dark countenance and eyes matched the black long-sleeved 3-button shirt stretched over his massive arms and chest. Dusky acid washed jeans faded into the shadows and muted his gray tennis shoes. All that was missing was the smell of brimstone.

He waited motionless, still as stone on a cathedral parapet waiting for Adrian to show up. Another one to remind of his always lapsing payment schedule. *The same, always the same*, rattled around by itself in his head, stirring up older memories, coating over older and then older still.

He had once hunted along Commercial Row and Lake Street to find his bosses' delinquent customers. They would flop at the Toscano Hotel and lounge around the horse book at the Turf Club touting whatever races they played. Many flew to that flame when Pappy Smith opened Harold's Club in 1935. Maybe it was the carnival familiarity of betting on the roulette wheel with a live mouse they came for. *You can take the boy out of the carney, but you can't take the carney out of the boy*.

"The carnival cons may really be the oldest profession after all," Tyrone said to no one in particular, and no one in particular paid much attention to the shadowy, hulking man of indeterminate age talking to himself at the table over by the wall. He melted into the plain coffee shop décor, like he was not there at all.

47

The unimaginative hustler looking for a bird's nest on the ground to set them up for life would naturally gravitate to Reno. Many held minor contracts with his boss they thought they could just skip on. It was low grade cash flow at the bottom of the food chain, but there was a lot of it. His bosses' business resembled Wal-Mart more than Nordstrom. There were always many more dumb crooks and lazy people looking for an easy score than those with real brains and talent – they owned the casinos the others played in.

The smarter hustlers made their own business success, and the ones with Tyrone's employer's help kept their contracts up to date. Some had gone south with Bugsy Siegel when he opened Las Vegas after taking over the Flamingo construction from William Wilkerson. The rest is the same history as Reno with brighter lights.

Lincoln Fitzgerald opened the Nevada Club in 1945 with *borrowed* Purple Gang money from the Jewish Mafia in Detroit. His unwilling Detroit bankers reminded him of his transgressions with a shotgun blast in his home driveway. It took special handling of Fitz's associates by the boss to retain him as a living customer. Tyrone had Fitz drop the police investigation to not disrupt the boss's cash flow. Fitz hid out in his casino for the remainder of his years, far away from his driveway.

East of Reno Joe Conforte ran the world infamous Mustang Bridge Ranch brothel that became legal in 1971. Tyrone went there over the years many times to find his customers. Joe ran another whorehouse before Bill Raggio arranged to have it burned down in 1960. Bill, a connected Washoe County DA went on to become a powerful Nevada legislator, while Conforte and his wife Sally ran The Mustang Ranch until the IRS closed it for good in 1999. Nevada is like that.

Jimmy Ing came from Anchorage, Alaska to take over the unlicensed business in Reno, including steal-to-order theft rings of luxury goods. He left an associate brain damaged with a baseball bat as an example to others to stay in line, when he wasn't beating his wife or burning others alive in barrels of oil – long before narco cartels and Draino. The police feared him and shot him at a phony stolen art sale west of town in 1967 – at least 22 times according to Joe Conforte who claimed the police set him up. There was nothing even the boss could do for him.

Tyrone's current deadbeats were different, and the same now. Reno morphed with the end of the last century into a Western U.S. drug hub for the Latin American narco cartels. Like the tax exempt warehouses of Nevada, the black tar heroin from Xalisco, meth, marijuana, and all the rest are distributed across the western states from Reno.

"Gangs are always the same," Tyrone muttered morosely. "No matter what language they speak, it's all the same fascination for easy fame and fortune." They came and went with every generation and all blurred together to him after awhile. He chased down the ones who were in arrears and tried to fix things when one or other of the slightly better customers got stupid, or greedy, or both. If they got smart and greedy and took out their competitors, Tyrone passed them along to the new business guys to upgrade their contracts. Upscale clients like Fitz always got a little extra service, they were worth it on average. None of them ever really learned though. They just got better or luckier at getting away with murder – which is why he got burned out on the job every decade or so. Jobs are like that.

Adrian sauntered into the food court with the oblivious self-importance that comes with the perceived street-smart knowledge of the whole real world. His vanity came with the smell of cooked grease and the cloying come-hither slot machine notes wafting between the brown laminated table outcroppings on the industrial gray paving stones. *Just another one of them*, Tyrone thought watching Adrian revel in the glances of the other fish in the noisy little puddle in the middle of the counterfeit carnival in the middle of the desert.

Tyrone's dead black eyes spiked Adrian in mid-stride. He subtly lifted his chin in a gesture of invitation and demand for Adrian to come over to join him on the edge of the food court. Adrian had never met Tyrone before, but his skittery instincts told him enough for him to carefully turn and scuttle away into the casino. "Oh, Adrian. No imagination. No brains." Tyrone said with a sigh as he stood up from his perch and walked quietly after the fleeing man. Few saw Adrian's feeble efforts to scurry away. They looked around to see who had spooked him lest it be somebody or some thing they might need to avoid. No one worth noting materialized so they turned back, believing he ran off to take care of some remembered business or other. The normal racket and lights accompanied the drifting Keno writers picking up tickets for the next game, flanked by mini-skirted cocktail hostesses trudging through the food court on their worn heels as the little ripples of disturbance subsided. Friday night went on.

Adrian darted out a back entrance onto West Street trying to walk away as nonchalantly as he could manage without running. He had just turned to hurry towards 4ᵗʰ Street when Tyrone suddenly appeared beside him and said, "Adrian, we need to speak about some issues you seem to have created with your account." Trapped between the looming figure and the wall of the casino he knew there was nowhere for him to run.

"What? What account you speaking to me about, güey? Do I know you, you talk to me like this?"

"Adrian, mi amigo, your success has been facilitated by the good contacts and benevolent conditions you have contracted for. You must comprehend those benefits are not without cost."

"Huh? What you are saying?"

"Pay. Adrian. It's time to pay. Now. Enough of your shit."

"Whoa, güey. I always pay. You know."

Tyrone saw the flicker of fear cross the small man's eyes before he rammed his thin shoulder into Tyrone's immobile bulk. He was quick though, and spun around on the rebound and ducked behind Tyrone's back before he could turn around. Adrian sprinted away between screeching, honking cars into the imagined safety of a darker neighborhood on the other side of the street. In Adrian's universe he knew he would be shot just as quickly on a busy sidewalk as running across a side street lawn, but at least it would be harder to hit him away from the bright light. He fumbled for his gun as he ran.

Tyrone followed without hesitation, weaving more carefully than Adrian through the perpetual car and foot traffic regardless of the time of day or the goings on that could interrupt their pilgrimage. Tyrone knew that it would be no use attracting attention by being knocked twenty feet in front of angry drivers and momentarily horrified pedestrians. He wove through the traffic and finally jogged into the shadows on the other side. The looky-loos turned back to their own concerns, ignoring the dim figure loping after the disappearing man.

Youth and adrenaline helped sallow Adrian sprint through empty parking lots into an area that was a mix of 1940's houses and low midcentury office buildings converted to professional service office space and shops, all closed for the night. Tyrone prepared to accelerate and catch Adrian to put an end to this when a fuzzy shape suddenly flashed out, snatching Adrian into the gloom before Tyrone could blink. Tyrone stopped instantly catching a blue glitter and saw six round, lidless eyes peering at him. Adrian's torn body fell to the ground and the shape darted away accompanied by a hiss and a scrabbling sound. He sensed whatever had grabbed Adrian had not been interested in him. He walked up to Adrian's twisted corpse lying on oil spotted asphalt under a dusty elm tree. Tyrone peered into the dim night, wondering what had killed Adrian.

He knew of many strange things between Heaven and Hell, but whatever had killed his debtor was not among them. Fear did not trouble Tyrone. *He will not be amused, I am sure. Hum, he is dissolving too.* The puddle of slime at his feet was all that remained of Adrian. "Adios, güey. You would have preferred to settle your debts with me rather than this, I'm quite sure," Tyrone said to the puddle. Business took priority over his curiosity, and Tyrone began calmly searching his phone memos for the next customer to visit. *The boss will have to figure it out. I will worry about it when I have more time.*

Tyrone ate at the Peppermill the following evening waiting for his next debtor to turn up. While he was eating an unfamiliar young woman in a business suit walked up to his table. She looked out of place a casino coffee shop. She stared straight at him as she entered the restaurant and approached his booth.

"Excuse me sir, may I have a word with you?"

"I believe it would be acceptable, miss. Please have a seat," Tyrone replied in an equally stiff way.

She sat across from Tyrone, her strong hands folded together. She leaned slightly forward and said: "Thank you. Whom do I have the honor of addressing?"

Hum, a forthright young woman, how refreshing on a tedious business trip. Kind of formal though. "You may call me Tyrone."

"And your last name?"

"Tyrone will suffice for now. And, you are?" A wry smile tickled the edges his wide lips.

"You may call me Ms. Garcia.

"Ha. That will work for me. I presume you came in search of me for a reason. What might that be?" Tyrone settled in to enjoy a conversation with someone more enlightened than the usual. Suspicion came automatically to him, but this was too interesting to pass up. He would play along for a while.

"I suspect you prefer me to be candid. The average person does find me easily, particularly when I am occupied with my profession. How did you manage?"

"Thank you. I can sometimes see things in the dark," the young woman said flatly.

"Hum, interesting, but not quite an answer. Again, what brings you to my table on this fine evening?"

"I was asked by an acquaintance to look you up. It seems you are not an *average person* either. He wants to understand more about you."

"Refreshing, Ms. Garcia." Stronger suspicion gave a cordial toothy smile to his game face. It met a tiny flicker of raised upper lip and crinkled nose in hers. *She really isn't afraid, only disgusted. That is interesting.*

"How do you know me, Ms. Garcia? I have the distinct impression there's more to this than just a chat over a meal about an inquisitive *friend*."

"I know of your business. We, my friend expected you. He may have been a little naïve, no, inexperienced, if that is even possible, to not expect you sooner given his recent behavior."

"Ah, now I understand," Tyrone said sitting back in his chair remembering the mysterious disposal of Adrian. "Your acquaintance has been stealing my customers in a most unsatisfactory way for my cash flow then."

"I hope no trouble comes from it for everyone's sake. I fear it won't be that way," she said with sad eyes. "I tried to tell my friend it would come to this, but he wouldn't listen. I suppose he's been here too long. It's understandable."

"So, where do we proceed to from here? We both have jobs to finish."

"I don't know," she said. She stood up and handed him her phone with a QR code on the screen for him to scan. "This will find me if you believe we can work something out. Maybe it's still possible." She waited while he scanned it into his phone and then walked away.

The code he scanned brought up a web page link for a Marlana Garcia, Attorney at Law, in Phoenix, Arizona. *Ah, Marlana. At least she trusts me with her first name.*

As Tyrone watched Marlana exit as he played through the meeting in his head. *There's no need to tell him right now about this threat. The bastard, "Why don't you go to Reno and clean up some of our arrears, you know it best. And, while you are there look into the issue I told you about." I should have known. Possibly she has a point though, if cooler heads can prevail.* He pulled up Calliope's contact.

Chapter 7

Cleveland, Ohio June 2014

The black glass walls of the Nationwide Professional Services Center building in downtown Cleveland bore no signage. The smooth rectangles covering dull mid-century monolith styling spoke no volumes and attracted no second looks.

Cally decided to exercise the system rather than walk into the building without bothering with the lobby. Henry was a stickler for process. The little tweak of showing up without an appointment would good for him, she thought. *He's the one with the problem.*

In the lobby white and black marble floors bounced sound brightly against standard average stainless steel elevator doors under tall ceilings. Yellowing plastic squares floated below the fluorescent lights. Brown fake wood paneled planters managed to keep the dusty, green plastic ivy looking almost alive while channeling any visitors towards the elevators. A gray uniformed security guard sitting half-hidden behind a planter watched a bank of black and white camera monitors lined across his white Formica table just in case something actually happened. Another gray sentinel waited at the reception desk in front of the elevators watching people walk by outside the tall tinted windows. Calliope went up to him.

"Excuse me, I am here to see Mr. Appleyard. Would you please call Loraine and tell her Ms. Dancer is here."

The guard took out his clipboard and ran his finger down the list of names. "I am sorry Miss …"

"Dancer, Ms. Dancer."

"Your name is not on the list. Are you sure that you have an appointment?"

"Mr. Appleyard will see me. Please call his administrator and tell her I am here."

The guard rarely saw visitors who were not on the list. Strict instructions forbade anyone from entering who was not on the list, salesmen most of all. "I am sorry, Miss Dancer, but what is your business here? You should contact the person you wish to see through our website and request an appointment with them. Mr. Appleyard does not see anyone without an appointment."

"Mr. Highland," Calliope said reading his nametag. "I am sure Loraine Carmichael will resolve this matter if you call her. Please call her at extension 3485 and tell her I am in the lobby. I would appreciate it. I'll wait over here." She smiled her best at the guard before walking over to the old fashioned angular chrome and black Naugahyd couch and chairs surrounding the low brown oval table with an old beige push button telephone on it to wait.

An elevator door opened and a middle-aged woman in a yellow skirt, light green shirt, and purple hair bounced out waving at Cally. "Hey there honey, so nice of you to drop by on us," she said loudly coming up behind the guard station. "Larry, please sign Calliope Dancer in and I will take her back."

Larry filled out the visitor log and Loraine took Calliope into the elevator.

"It's nice to see you dear," Loraine said with a big smile. "I told him you were here and ran down to get you. He'll be fussing about it you know. He just hates when somebody doesn't follow the rules. He'll start reminding me again about scheduling things properly and how 'it costs money to interrupt my work for these unnecessary intrusions, Loraine.'"

"It's good for him. Besides, he contacted me, to tell me to make an appointment and that he would not pay for anything."

"Of course he did. He's doing the accounting for the quarter and not happy about something. I suspect it's why he reached out to you in the first place. What's going on?"

"I just don't know yet Loraine. I wish I did."

"Oh yes, big business I know. I can keep a secret."

"Yes, you have to in this office, and I'd tell you except now I am still feeling around in the dark myself."

"Okay, I get it. Don't worry about it."

Loraine poked her head into an office across from her desk. "Mr. Appleyard, Ms. Dancer is here to see you," she said through the doorway.

"No wait! I told you she does not have an appointment. I am very busy and she needs to call first," came from inside.

"I'll keep her at my desk and we'll catch up until you're free to see her," Loraine said with a wink at Calliope and a quick step with her over to her desk.

"No, I told you – damn, damn, damn," came the reply.

Before they could sit down a dark little man with a receding hairline and deep brown eyes and a blue three-piece suit, white shirt, and red tie sprang out of the office. "Well, since you're here you might as well come in. I can give you a few minutes of my time." Thin pursed lips accompanied his quick little headshake and insistent hand motions to come over to his office.

"Miss Dancer, I thought you would call to schedule an appointment. I suppose since you are here, come in, come in. I can spare a little time, though I am very busy. This is a terrible interruption," he said quickly gesturing her into the office, almost hopping to get things moving.

"Hold my calls, Loraine. This won't take long," Appleyard shouted to his administrator before closing the door.

"Yes, Mr. Appleyard."

"Time is money Loraine," Cally said quickly, causing Loraine to stifle a laugh.

"That will be quite enough," he said closing the door behind them. "Sit down and tell me what you are here for."

"A big bird told me you were losing paying customers."

"I can guess who that might be, but never mind. A business does not run itself; little things grow into big things when you don't pay attention. Good customers do not grow on trees, especially those with cash potential."

"So, you are losing customers, good ones too."

"Possibly. You understand, this is proprietary information not to be bandied about with any Tom, Dick, or Harry you sit in a bar with Miss Dancer. We have a non-disclosure agreement with you ..."

"Yes Henry, I'm aware. I keep all my clients' affairs private, even without one of your 30 page *standard* non-disclosures," Cally said before he could continue. "Even when I'm drunk at a hotel bar with that traveling FBI agent I met last night."

"Always a joke, always a joke with you. This is a business meeting you came for," he said, this time with a cold hiss and steely eyes.

"Very good. You *are* serious about this. Now we can talk. Let me began with what I learned and then you can fill in the rest. If I can help you, and we can agree on what my role should be, I am happy with the same arrangements we had recently for your fast food business. My efforts to stop the mayor from forcing people to diet by drinking smaller sodas resolved itself once everybody discussed it and you helped him raise campaign contributions in your special way. I'm glad to have been able to help you."

"Yes, I suppose your machinations did save me the time and expense of a more forceful undertaking with that do-gooder. It was almost worth your exorbitant hourly rate. Let's see where we are at on this. It might save some expense if you can get to the bottom of it. Go on with your story and perhaps we can come to an arrangement if it will significantly benefit my business."

Calliope ignored his cheapskate comment and proceeded to tell him about disappearing clients and her trip to the underground in France. She decided to leave out the gossip from Clarence until she could figure out if it meant anything.

"Yes, yes we wondered what became of that up and coming young man. He showed so much promise," Appleyard said when she finished. " … and that delightful young woman in Portland who had her life cut tragically short."

"Last evening we lost a customer right in front of our eyes. He was not the best customer you understand, but the events were nonetheless shocking. We could not do anything for him as it happened so fast. It was an unfamiliar event for us, and the details of what happened are very confusing," he continued

"Interesting, what do you know about it?"

"I suggest you call your *big bird* and ask him. He was involved, but he can't seem to get very far on it. Yes, I need to – well, he is one of the best, but his head has not been in the game recently. And he had a vacation six years ago. No, never mind, you just worry about what this is about before we lose any more," Mr. Appleyard said half to Calliope and half to himself.

Calliope did fill in some details of a few more instances she had heard bits and pieces about through her network, but not much else.

"I'll be in touch," Calliope said standing up when it was clear Appleyard was not going to tell her anything more. "My invoices will be submitted to … "

"No no no, you send them to Loraine directly. I want to see them first before accounts payable. I know how you consultants charge. I don't expect to see any of your outrageous expenses sneaking through accounting, Miss Dancer."

"My expenses will be proper. You know that. I'll bill you if you want extra paperwork on all of them to explain everything in detail. Do you?"

"No no, you just send them to Loraine and manage the costs. That will be sufficient for now."

"Thank you for your time."

"Yes yes, let me know as soon as you settle this." Mr. Appleyard said, turning back to his quarterly accounting with a sneering pout and a backhanded "go along now" wave to Calliope without looking up.

"You get a green eye shade for your stocking this Christmas," Calliope said quietly with a smile.

"Yes. Goodbye."

"She lives," Loraine said as Calliope came out of her bosses' office. "Check your wallet."

"Yup, I did. He wants me to send my invoices through you."

"Oh, it's important if he is going to *pay you* for it. Want to tell me about it now?" Loraine said raising her eyebrows.

"I promise to tell you what I can when I understand it myself."

"I'll hold you to it," Loraine said with a pout.

"I will, I promise."

"Okay then. Wait, I will walk you out," Loraine said getting up to walk with Calliope to the lobby.

Chapter 8
Phoenix, Arizona June 2014

The outdoor thermometer on the marquee of the Paradise Valley Mall in Scottsdale, Arizona, read "114°" while Calliope waited in the food court next to the granite boulders. She did not care for being in Arizona during the baking summer, but Tyrone had told her the story of his encounter in Reno with the deadly creature and the visit from the mysterious lawyer. It was all she had to go on, meaning a trip to Phoenix in June to meet with her. At least the mall had powerful air conditioning and the splashing water on the rock decorations gave a feeble illusion of cool and wet.

Marlana's office turned out to be a mail center with a bank of post office boxes. Her mobile number went directly to voice mail when Cally tried it. The Go Daddy hosted website had the online Whois record for finding the owner of the website domain blocked. It only listed the address of the rented mailbox, a domain email, and the same mobile number for contacting the owner. Google was no help either. There were many Marlana Garcias. The Arizona Bar Association showed Marlana as an active member, but the address, phone, and fax numbers were the same as the website.

Calliope had left a message on the office phone to request a meeting. She received a text back with a time, date, and directions to the food court in the mall.

Marlana's clicking dress heels accompanied the trickling from the boulders when she came up to shake hands with Calliope. She wore dark business formal even in the Phoenix summer. Both women smiled, exchanged polite greetings, and careful appraisals. Calliope had dressed casually in white pants, a light blue patterned shirt, and mirrored sunglasses that she took off when Marlana came up to her.

Calliope was a little unnerved how Marlana spotted her instantly across the cavernous food court and walked right up to her. *I didn't give her much of a description either. I wonder if she was already here waiting for me – or has somebody else here too?* Calliope thought looking around herself.

"Thank you for meeting with me on short notice, Ms. Garcia. I took the liberty of ordering a latte to accompany a tiny snack. Actually, it is something I make myself for these trips, would you like one?" Calliope said offering the other woman a chocolate coconut trifle.

"You are welcome. I am surprised you got here so fast, given air travel today. Oh, and thank you. I just had lunch but I will save it for later," Marlana said, putting the candy in a napkin and into her purse before Calliope could respond. "Where is it you said you came in from again?"

"My office is in San Francisco, but I was visiting a client in the Midwest when I called you. I just switched my tickets around and showed up here. Too much business travel lately."

"Yes, Sky Harbor is my second home sometimes. I am happy you could get here overnight. Even I have trouble doing that," Marlana said with a big smile.

"I understand, SFO knows me well." *I bet she checked flights. It won't help.*

"Well, what can I do for you Ms. Dancer? It's your dime. You said you were investigating a missing person in Nevada and I might be able to help you? I told you I am just a busy attorney in Arizona, but you insisted it was something that was better done in person than over the phone."

"I believe you met one of my client's sales reps in Reno a few days ago. I am here to see if there are things you might want to clear up about that business." *Might as well be direct and get to the point with her. My, what a poker face she has. Ice in her.*

"Umm, yes I believe I met your client's man there. So, you are his response?"

"I am an agent who does not want to see people do rash things or harm another's business interests. Forgive my directness, but I believe you are of the same mind, at least you indicated the same when you spoke with Tyrone."

Marlana stared hard at Calliope for a moment before responding. "Ms. Dancer, I am worried about what can happen when things get out of hand. I have a client also, whose interests are possibly not all that much different from yours. But I can only advise my client, not make decisions for him nor am I permitted to take any significant actions without his express approval. You may actually have more latitude than I do."

Calliope wished Marlana had had her special. *But maybe this will still yield something significant. How do I get her to trust? I have to go with it and see what happens.*

"You can call me Calliope," she said with an almost genuine smile. "Tyrone is somebody I trust. He has a difficult job sometimes and sees many odd things in his work. You surprised him, that's all, Ms. Garcia."

"Marlana. Please go on."

"Marlana. Well, he saw something out of even his ordinary last week. You then visited him the next day at his job site, if you will. He is one who connects the dots, so his interest was piqued. Long story short, his employer asked me to see if there was more to all that than coincidence.

"I see we are both professionals in our business. We both have our client's best interests at heart. And, given your conversation with Tyrone, and the violence of the incident he witnessed, we may be working for the same ends albeit from different sides."

"My client does not want bad things to happen to his business, but I'm still a little at a loss about who exactly you represent and what it's all about for that matter. I'm still getting my feet on the ground about all this, so anything you can tell me will be very helpful. I can then help my client understand and we can calm things down together," Calliope said with a smile.

"I had hoped for more. Is that what we are here for?" Marlana replied after a brief pause.

Calliope saw a tiny cool flash from Marlana and a firm set come briefly to her lips.

Damn, damn, I am losing her.

Marlana sat silently for a moment before saying with a tinge of anger coming into her voice, "Ca ... Ms. Dancer, your client, well I'm sorry. Things happen in *business* and adjustments have to be made. It's not always predictable, *is it*? Please convey that there should not be any issue arise that could complicate things further. I apologize, but I have another meeting to attend."

Marlana then stood abruptly, shook hands, and walked away before Calliope could respond.

Calliope was stunned. Her charm and ability to extract information from people deserted her completely with Marlana, even without the help of her chocolates. She thought she had her for a moment and then, poof, she was gone.

She sat for a moment next to the water splashing on the rocks without hearing it or the escaped children scampering around it. Marlana knew what Tyrone had seen, and it felt like she even understood the *business* Calliope had with Tyrone and Appleyard. Marlana didn't like Calliope meddling in it all, if Calliope judged her correctly. *That unintentional anger was real. It irritated her to have let it slip out from behind her poker face. Now what?*

***

Calliope took a hotel room at the Scottsdale Marriot overnight to think about her next move.

The temperature had dropped to a balmy 106° with the threat of a monsoon brewing by the time she had set herself up by the Marriot pool with a Mai Tai and a swimsuit she bought at the mall. She punched in a number on her mobile phone after a sip of her second drink and a bite of a Macadamia Cluster morsel to help her unwind in the warm air for a moment. *I am going to need some help on this.*

Coppersmith Associates had their headquarters in London. Calliope worked with their San Francisco office and they gave her contact information for a local Phoenix PI firm when she explained her desire to track down an attorney in the Phoenix area.

Alan Corwin of Corwin Investigations took her call himself and offered to come by the Marriot to meet with her.

"Now, what is it I can do for you?" Alan said after they took a table in the bar by the pool.

"Thank you, Mr. Corwin, for meeting with me. To be brief, I need information about a local attorney who represents a potential client. Her name is Marlana Garcia and here is the information I have," Calliope said, handing him a piece of hotel notepaper with Marlana's name, description, mail box, website, mobile phone number, and email address on it. "I would like to find out as much as I can about her quickly so I can decide whether to proceed with the relationship. I do not need an exhaustive investigation, just a good basic set of information for right now. I am not too familiar with Phoenix, and Richard Coppersmith said you were just the person to help me. I trust his judgment."

"It sounds very doable. What else can you tell me about her to get started?"

"Well, I am afraid not much, which is why I contacted you. Her name is Marlana Garcia, she is listed with the Arizona Bar, and well, that's about it. Just what's on the paper."

This is it?" Alan said looking at the information on the note again. "A young Hispanic woman, about 30-35, 5'8", slim, black hair and brown eyes. A mobile phone, PO box, and a website email as her address? I see why you called. Don't you have anything else? Do you know anything about where she might be found, anything?"

"I wish I did, but I've only met her once, today in a shopping mall. She left before I could find out very much at all about her. I didn't think to follow her to her car, but to be honest I really don't think she's the kind of person who wouldn't have been aware of me doing it, if you catch my drift."

"Yes, yes I do. I think we can do something in any case. That's our business. Did you have a chance to look at the terms and conditions of our service I emailed you?

"Yes I did. It sounds acceptable. If you will give me a short fixed price proposal electronically for a one-week engagement, I'm prepared to authorize it and EFT you a binder. Is that acceptable to you?"

"Yes, that'll work fine." He had expected a larger contract, without such a short turn around, and not fixed price either. Richard Engle had called him directly to tell him Calliope Dancer was one of his best clients and to do whatever she needed. Maybe he could sell her more after this little pissant job was over.

***

Alan seethed on the telecom with Calliope a week later. She had held him to the original contract, and he had to put extra people on it in addition to having to buy information from people at Marlana's mobile service just to find out what little he had. This asshole lawyer was a ghost. He had also spent money investigating Calliope just to run into similar walls, except she appeared to be very well connected with some movers and shakers in a lot of places. It did not help that Richard Engle called him again to tell him to mind his own business about her after he called Coppersmith Associates through back channels to check up on her. Richard ordered him "just do the work he agreed to" for her. The bitch really pissed him off.

"Yes, Ms. Dancer, that's all I have. She comes from here in Phoenix; her grandfather came from Mexico and ran a little barrio mercado that her father turned into a local chain of three small supermarkets. She was a party girl at Arizona State until a criminal gang extorted her father to steal his business. He tried to resist them by himself, and one store was burned and customers were harassed at others. The business fell apart. He lost everything and died in an automobile accident a few years later.

"Marlana graduated with a degree in communications and C+ grades at about the time of the fire. She went into the law school at Arizona State University four years later. She passed the bar in Florida and went to work for a firm called Salvatore, Arthur, and Reynolds, with offices in Miami and San Francisco. She was accepted to the bar in Arizona about a year ago. She has clients for the firm she serves in Arizona as far as we can tell."

"Thank you, Alan," Calliope said. "What kind of clients does Marlana have? What is her practice about?"

"It seems to be general business clients, setting up small businesses, personal family matters, things like that," Alan said. He did not tell her he made up this part. The law firm in Florida was very closed to prying eyes and guarded their client list rigorously. He had found very little about Marlana and her Florida employer.

"What can you tell me about her? What does she like or do?"

"She's a typical young lawyer, works long hours and goes out drinking with others from the firm after work, as far as we have seen," he continued to lie.

"So, you have followed her? You must have seen more? Has she met with anybody in particular?"

"Well, yes, she's not into much outside work. It's only been a week we have been on the case. Her meetings looked like general business lunches over drinks. We could find out much more if we had more time."

"Did you recognize anybody in particular that she met with, or in any unusual places? Any photographs."

"Hum, yes, our agent only had a cell phone camera and was a little too far away to get any good pictures, but we can do more with the right equipment and some more time."

"Thank you so much, Alan. For right now this is a lot to mull over. I will come back and have you do more if I need it after I digest this information. I will tell Richard that you were very helpful."

"I appreciate it, Ms. Dancer. I always enjoy the people Richard introduces me to. Do stay in touch if there is anything more we can do for you."

"Thanks again. Bye now," Cally said hanging up.

"Yeah, 'bye now' like you'll fucking call back," Alan muttered when he hung up. "And the ass pain lawyer Jesus never could find. What does she expect in a fucking week."

***

Calliope had one of her new batch of cherry surprises with her mint chocolate latte to help her think about what to do now after hanging up with the useless Phoenix PI. She had expected him to find out more than just a few school records and newspaper stories about the opaque Marlana. But she wasn't really surprised either. *This whole thing is like this. One turn after another into a blind alley, or sewer main.*

Cally dialed her old friend Al Gonzales. She had done him a good turn when he was investigated after resigning as Attorney General. He had gone back into private practice in Tennessee and might be able help find some information about the invisible woman.

***

"Good evening, Miss Dancer," the deep Texas drawl began through the earpiece when Calliope answered her phone back in San Francisco. "I called to see if I might be able to help you out on a little problem you're having with a lady lawyer."

"Oh, thank you for calling. I was told someone might contact me, you must be him, Mr. ... " Calliope said leaning back in her office chair.

"Wayne, but you can call me John." *You left out 'little lady' John*, Cally thought smiling.

"Did you get a text today about an email account? Do you have it?"

"Yes I did. So I should look in the email draft folder for the account?"

"Yes ma'am. Use Tor secure browser for it if you don't mind. Do you know it?"

"That won't be a problem. Is there anything you need to tell me first?"

"I do believe you'll find what you need in the email folder Ma'am."

"Thank you so much. And pass along that I am sure this will be very helpful and I appreciate it. Sorry that politics is such a nasty business."

"Yep, it's a blood sport. There're rodents in the walls lotsa times, Ma'am. Take care now."

"I will Mister Wayne. Bye now."

"Gu'night lit-ele lady."

Calliope laughed, and could hear the smile over the line as it clicked off.

The Tor browser opened an email account with a message in the draft folder:

Subject:
Marlana Garcia:
Female, 38, 5'7", black/brown,
Hispanic (Mexican/Chilean)
US Citizen
3161 Naples Road, #16
Miami, FL 33017

and-

247 Shiprock Street #A38
Phoenix, AZ 85011
FLDL # C321896k

PP#
340000230USA50010M1101236902
000002<140750
Recent, 1 year: Mexico, Brazil, Argentina, Chile, Canada,

China
Languages: English, Spanish (fl),
some: Portuguese, Chinese

Education: ASU: BA,
Communications, GPA 2.67 (2000)
ASU Law: JD, GPA 3.92,
Law Review (2007)

Admitted to Bar: 2007 Florida, 2009
Arizona – practicing
Senior associate, Salvatore, Arthur,
and Reynolds
LLP, Miami (2007)
1 Century Circle
Ste. 201
Miami, FL 33013

Analysis:
SA&R is a corporate firm with clients
in China, Australia, EU, North and South
America. Clients range from Fortune 250 to
high net worth individuals. SA&R also does
government business for US, Brazil and Chile.
The firm is solely owned by the named
partners and client lists are close hold. They
shun any media coverage. Business is mostly
long term existing clients and few new clients.
They have no litigation or criminal defense
practice.
Subject reports to Carmine Salvatore
directly. Carmine handles investments for an
unknown number of high net worth
individuals and several hedge funds based in
and outside of the US, primarily in
Asia/Pacific. He is unknown in Miami social
circles, does not play golf or attend public

events. The firm is his life and his only interest outside it is sporting clays, which he indulges in at a private shooting range at his gated Miami area home. He entertains clients there, but does not hold any social or family events there.

Subject travels for Carmine to visit his clients and for private business events. Subject has received training at the Executive Protection Institute, Paul Ekman Group, and the Public Agency Training Council. Subject is skilled at situational awareness and managing her public profile in a secure manner.

Subject has traveled to Nevada (Reno: 5 June-9 June, Las Vegas: 13 July), Arizona (Phoenix: 9-June-10 July), and California (San Francisco: 10 July-13 July) in the last 60 days. Current whereabouts are presumed near Las Vegas (unconfirmed, unused return flight).

Note:
Subject took family business loss hard (1997). Father resisted a Russian organized crime move into Arizona food service and credit racketeering in low-income neighborhoods where the family operated grocery stores (3). Stores were vandalized and arson was suspected against one property. Insurance carrier delayed payment to the family claim on the property as a result.

Subject's father, Hector Garcia, died in a one-car accident (1998). Autopsy determined blood alcohol content of 0.23. Wife abandoned heavily indebted family home to return to native Chile with Subject. Remaining business properties put into foreclosure and litigation outside of bankruptcy by the insurance carrier. Lien holders opened litigation in Chile and US against wife and daughter as presumptive heirs.

Banks and insurance carrier resolved disputes when properties sold to Tripartate Limited Holdings, a Cayman Islands corporation with suspected organized crime connection(s) (2000).

Subject returned to US 22 months later to attend law school at ASU (2004).

Subject joined SA&R 2007.

See attached.

"Sheesh, she was in San Francisco the day after I came back from Phoenix. I do have to find this woman again. I do like Las Vegas. I wonder if Steve Wynn has a room for me?" Calliope said to herself, staring at the email.

The attachments included photographs of Marlana, her mother, and father, as well as news clippings about the fire and her father's accident. Separate enclosures contained copies of her various training and education certificates, passport, driver's license, corporate email, personal email, and personal cell phone number. A third file held copies of the litigation proceedings, sales records, and links to Tripartate Limited Holdings' public face. The fourth file had copies of Marlana's airline tickets, rental cars, and lodging for the listed travel. The last bit gave a Travelodge in Henderson, Nevada as her last known location, unconfirmed.

"I do believe Al still has some of his contacts," Calliope said finishing the attachments. "I owe him some special candy for this."

Chapter 9

Calliope wanted to take her new bicycle to Las Vegas, but adding the front and rear panniers would just ruin the elegant lines of the Gitane racer. There were no mounting points on the thin carbon fiber frame for them either. She needed a real touring bicycle to schlep all her gear to the desert. The Koga-Miyata World Traveler fit the bill nicely. She didn't worry too much about how well it rolled on gravel or even pavement.

The trip to Las Vegas did not compare to the crossing from Paris. Calliope took the scenic route over to the Sierra Nevada Mountains, down the ridge to Death Valley, and a left-turn to Las Vegas.

The gaudy display of Colorado River electricity in dancing neon dazzled as she swerved to avoid the Luxor searchlight and the tourist helicopters zooming over the neon road through Paradise.

Calliope chose a low-key room at Harrah's under an assumed name rather than a suite at one of Steve Wynn's hotels. In fact, she did not tell him or anyone else she was coming to Las Vegas.

The hotel begrudgingly allowed her bulging bicycle up to the room through a freight elevator arranged by the valet. He had stopped her when she started to wheel it into the lobby to register. She leaned the bike on the wall at the foot of the king size bed and looked out at the High Roller observation wheel slowly spinning next to the Flamingo. Calliope had a lime crème, a hot shower, and went to bed. Tomorrow she planned to visit Marlana's Henderson motel and start getting to the bottom of things. *Oh well, next time I come here it will be for fun.*

Calliope played tourist and took a cab to the east side of Henderson to find Marlana's motel. The newish brown paint on the stucco set off by almost clean green doors matched the empty parking lot and gang graffiti on the dumpsters peeking out from the end of the two story prison block motif. No trees or other living things disturbed the industrial gray asphalt expanse in front nor the empty lots running off towards Lake Meade in the back. Darkness formed a black background for sodium vapor light pools warming the pavement in orderly yellow splotches. Calliope paid the dark cab driver in the navy blue turban, who had been telling her about how strange Americans were because they did not all live with their families and how much he missed his own here in Las Vegas. He asked her if she was sure she wanted to be dropped off out here before heading back to the airport to get in line for his next fare.

The desk clerk to showed up eventually behind the thick bulletproof glass in the tiny harsh, white lobby with the bare fluorescent tubes, after repeated call button jabs and shouts from Calliope.

"Yes, you want room?" the middle-aged Asian woman with a sour pout said. "You only ring bell one time," she snapped.

"Oh, I was afraid you were closed and nobody was here," Calliope said with her biggest fake smile. "I came to meet one of your guests."

"I don't rent you room to meet people one hour. Go somewhere else for that," the woman said turning away.

"No wait, I am looking for one of your guests. I have a meeting with her."

"What? One of guests call you? A woman? I not want that in my place."

"No, no I have, she is a friend I have not seen since we went to high school together. I am meeting here to go out and see a show at Caesar's. It is not *that* kind of thing. I am not here to entertain her. She is an old friend," Cally said quickly while reaching into her purse for her wallet.

"You police then? You have badge?" the surly clerk said watching Cally's hands.

"No, not police. I am here to see my friend Marlana Garcia. She gave me room number 19 and there was nobody there when I knocked. Maybe you can tell me the right one so we can start our vacation," she said pulling out two twenty-dollar bills. How does she get into the place to knock on the door if she has to be buzzed in at the front?

"Hum, Okay, let me look room up," the clerk said after a sneer and a hard look at Calliope. She laid her hand, palm up in the steel tray under the thick glass first.

"She in room 38 in back. I not see her two days. I have security camera, no funny stuff," she said walking away with the money.

Quiet rooms behind the motel looked like the ones in front: green, brown, and gray. A few more oil stains on the gray and a view of sand and weeds instead of Highway 95 in the distance. A dusty white Yukon with black desert windows parked near the front end as Calliope came around the building. An off-gray Toyota gone purple under the yellow light listed in front of the only room with light peeking around the black out drapes near the middle of the building.

Staccato thunder shattered the stillness when Calliope walked up to knock on door #38 towards the end of the building. Three blinding white lights dazzled her and the wall of the motel as the machines roared up and thunked silent.

No light came from the room and nobody came to the door. Cally turned and walked into the white light.

"Hi," she said. "I seem to have lost my friend here in Room 38. I was wondering if you've seen her."

A fat rider with the graying bush around his face smiled and answered. "Nope, we have not seen anybody in that room." He left his headlight on and went to pound his fist on the door with the Toyota in front. The other two riders glared at Calliope and said nothing. The blond one with deep lines in his thin face said, "Get lost. Now."

"Okay," she said with a shrug and a smile. She turned and quickly walked around the nearest end of the building where the green graffiti covered dumpsters sat – right into the arms of an armored SWAT officer with a night vision eyepiece. He clamped a hand over her mouth and dragged her to the front side of the motel. Five police cruisers waited there next to a black tactical van surrounded by black troopers fanning out to the opposite ends of the structure. The officer handed her off to another who told her to remain silent. He took her purse, wire tie cuffed her, and hustled her into the van. Another sat her on a bench to wait next to her with his M4 rifle across his chest and a gloved finger across the trigger guard.

"What's going on, officer," she said leaning forward to see if he had a nameplate.

"Please wait quietly Ma'am," he said through his black balaclava, glancing at her. "You will be able to speak with an officer shortly. This is for your own safety."

She did not waste her breath saying anything else. *Never a dull moment on this case. I wonder if they're after Marlana too?*

There were no shooting bursts, only the sounds of doors slamming and cars driving away outside the van to pass the time. The squawking of her guard's radio seemed routine. From what she could tell from the lack of excitement on the radio, it sounded like the police action went without violence. Finally, a regular uniformed officer opened the door to the rear of the van and looked up at her.

"Thanks, Franco. Looks like we got zip. Fucking swatted. What's this?" he said nodding at Calliope.

"That's for you, Michael. I'm just the babysitter," he said standing up and dropping the rifle down his chest on the strap with his finger still across the trigger guard.

"Do you have any identification?" Franco asked Calliope.

"Yes, but I seem to be tied up at the moment," she said with a chuckle.

"Oh, here is what we found on her," the SWAT officer said handing her purse to Michael as he helped Cally down the steps of the van and through the ring of black figures to the waiting patrol car. They started filing into the van as Michael led her behind the car where a short female officer with sergeant chevrons waited. He handed the sergeant the purse and stood behind Calliope with a hand on her elbow.

"… couple of pissed off Mongols from Boulder … cheap hookers in room … bullshit call … what's her story …" drifted by in snatches from the SWAT team as they walked past.

The sergeant set the purse on the trunk beside an evidence bag and took over. "I am going to search you for weapons, Ma'am," she said to Calliope.

"Am I under arrest?" Calliope said, receiving no answer from either officer.

"Officer Daimler I am searching the suspect's purse for weapons."

Boy I'm glad I left the SIG in my room tonight, Calliope thought.

"Now Ma'am please identify yourself."

"My name is Calliope Dancer. Are you arresting me?"

"Please tell me why you are here tonight?"

"Please release my hands if you are not arresting me. You have not found any weapons. I do not represent a threat."

"You were handcuffed for your own safety and the safety of the police in a dangerous situation. Please tell me why you were here tonight." The sergeant made no motion to release Calliope.

"Are you arresting me Sergeant?"

"We cannot determine that until you tell me why you are here."

"Are you arresting me? Please remove my restraints."

"I need to know why you were here to make that determination," the sergeant said sternly with a cold look at Calliope while Michael squeezed her elbow tightly from behind.

" Sergeant ... Clarke," Cally said reading her name. "Am I under arrest?"

"Put her in the car, Michael. And take off the cuffs. Hand me your driver's license from your bag."

Calliope sat in the back of the police car rubbing her wrists while Sergeant Clarke ran her driver's license.

"You are free to go, Ms. Dancer," she said coming around to open the rear door next to Calliope. "I suggest you leave."

"I need to call a cab."

"I would wait in the office. Goodnight, Ms. Dancer."

Calliope walked across to the motel office searching for a taxi number on her phone browser. She found a cab posting on Yelp and called for a ride. The SUV with the black windows rolled smoothly from behind the motel and turned out on the street heading in the direction of Las Vegas.

Calliope waited inside the little white refrigerator lobby for her cab and had a lime crème to calm down. The surly desk clerk never materialized, and Calliope had no interest in calling her. She felt all the evening's excitement had finally petered out; no more motorcycles, police cruisers, or anything else crawled in from the night to visit upon her. She ducked out of the lobby to the desert side of the motel when she was sure the police were gone. She walked nonchalantly out into the desert away from the light, before walking up and over to The Strip.

The angry cab driver pounded on the thick glass and jammed the call button after driving around the lot three times and banging on Room 38 the first time around. Nobody came to argue with him and he stomped out slamming the door of his Prius taxi, before stomping down the gas pedal to quietly scatter gravel around the parking lot on his way back to town.

***

"What happened there, Sergeant?"

"We got swatted. The call came from her phone."

"What! And you did not take her in? What's up with that?"

"I got a direct order from the lieutenant to bounce her. Said no arguing, he had his orders from the captain. Let it go, he said."

"How'd he get it?"

"I called it to the lieutenant before we brought her in because it was a bad SWAT call."

"That sucks. Who quashed it you think?"

"No idea. Probably Chief Daniels knows her from Cleveland or something. Or she has something with the DA. I just don't like this. Somebody coulda' got killed."

"If it was Ponzio, he'll have a time with those bikers. They were armed and had meth in the room with the hookers, but their lawyer will bitch we had no PC to bust 'em."

"Yeah, let him worry about it. I still hate these things, and when we know who it was too. Fucking politics."

***

Cally walked up The Strip beside the line of slowly moving cars, dodging tourists hurrying between hotels in the hot summer night. Thermometers read 101 degrees at 12:47 AM, warning people it was far better to stay in synthetic cities under painted clouds than brave the sidewalks and traffic in the desert heat even at night.

She wracked her brain about what to do next. Marlana, her only lead in this pointless engagement without substance came and went like the Cheshire Cat, only her smile visible when she wished it. *Who are YOU Ms. Garcia, and where's that fucking Rabbit who knows everything?* She drifted over to the edge of the sidewalk staring at her phone to make a call.

She ended up staring at the ponderous wheel creep around in dark gray sky with no stars, shrouded by the frantic glare of lights all competing with each other to be the most cool, grand, and expensive all at the same time. Roller coaster rumble, fountain splashing, car starting, and faint buzz-crackle neon sounds mixed with an undertone of people noises and faint clink of bells ringing escaping through air curtains. The white noise soothed her tired mind as she watched the slow wheel roll up into the charcoal gray sky. She tipped her head back to stare straight up at a few lonely stars twinkling in almost black. Cool fell over her face from the sky while the heat from the hot sidewalk tried to lift her up to it. An upside down world where cities were inside in constant daytime, while outside night coolness came down from the sky with heat rising up from the ground, and never quite nighttime at all.

"What'cha lookin' at Calliope? The saucers are in the basement of the Luxor, not up there," a cheerful voice said beside her.

She jerked back from her reverie to see an elegant woman with blond hair forming a perfect vertical cataract behind her upturned face standing beside her.

"No wait, I see one now. Hey, hey we're down here, come and get us quick!" she shouted waving at the sky.

"Ha, Veronica Tait, as I live and breathe. Y'all never did go back to Texas after all," Calliope said smiling. "Still the same smart ass, too. I am glad you dragged yourself out to see me."

"Now Calliope, you never did go back to Sacramento after all either. Nice place to be from, if I remember high school. God save me."

"Yes, we both got out alive. It's nice to see you Veronica. You look great." Cally said looking up and down the tall figure in a designer mini dress on 6-inch

Italian pumps smiling at her with perfect white teeth, flawless white skin, and sparkling light blue eyes.

"If you knew what it costs, and not even counting the hours in the gym and the hunger pains. My dentist and cosmetic surgeon both have vacation homes in Tahoe off of me."

"Where did the Air Force send your father after McClellan?"

"Anchorage, Alaska. It's near Hell; turn south at Sarah's Wasilla. I went to community college there for a year, got a ticket on Alaska Airlines and escaped the gulag to LA. Dad stayed out his last enlistment and retired back to Austin. I thought he would stay up there. It was his kind of people, but he never did like the cold. What did you do after Sackatomato?"

"I went to Davis, and then got an MBA at Stanford. Mom and dad are in Auburn now, but I don't get there very often. I'm in San Francisco, but travel a lot for my work."

"Sounds familiar. I live in Vegas, but travel wherever the whales want."

"What do you do? Not consulting I hope."

"Entertainment." Veronica said turning her palms up and looking down at her tiny dress. "Now, why did you call me, I'm happy to see you again though?"

"Oh, I see. Well, it is not all that different from consulting, is it now. I am stuck on this strange case. I guess that is what you call it. It's not the usual business lubrication engagement I normally do. Like you, I schmooze with movers and shakers in their world and help them keep their scams going for one more day. When they have a problem, I want them to call me first. You can't believe the bizarre things I have seen."

"Ha, Calliope I bet I can," Veronica said with a cynical laugh.

"I hear you. So, maybe you can point me in the right direction on this. I need somebody who lives here who will tell me if they have seen anything strange, is the best way to put it. Strange. I also need to find someone, an attorney named Marlana Garcia, who seems to be connected to all this and is here, or at least was here a few days ago. I expect something happened that I need to find out about if she came here."

Calliope went on to fill in Veronica in broad terms about disappearing criminals, that she had a client "back East" who lost a family member in the middle of all this and wanted to find out what happened, and that Marlana popped up in the same place as some of the disappearances. She seemed to know something about those, even if she could not get anything out of her when they had a meeting.

"Whew, I see what you mean," Veronica said. "It isn't much information is it? This is Las Vegas. If you watch TV, there's a bizarre murder like these every day here. But for now I have to go think about this. I have no clue about this Marlana person, or where to start either. I need to get back to you if I can come up with anything, okay?"

"Sure, that's fine. I took a shot that somebody local might have heard something or other."

"Are you staying in town?"

"I can, and still have to decide what to do next. I'm staying at Harrah's, Room 648 under Anne Baker. And you have my cell?"

"Yes I do. Let me ask around and get back to you in a day or two."

"Okay, thank you. I really appreciate this; anything you find is more than I have now. And, the next time I have to go to Paris I will be sure to call you."

"That sounds great, Calliope, you're on."

Weariness assailed Calliope all at once. The night became gritty and harsh, the luminous funhouse strident. Illusions cracked, exposing too many people, lights, and buildings planted in the middle of a hot desert night, toughing out another graveyard shift to get a moment of cool dawn. She trudged towards her room.

***

"She's done with whoever she met with. ... Yeah, played tourist, you should be able to ID her. ... Okay, looks like Harrah's. ... Yeah, that's how we found her. It was a pain. Glad you had those photos. ... Yeah, I'll confirm. ... You want me to wait till she comes out? ... Okay, better she sits around all night in the lobby than me. ... Yeah, I'll write it up in the morning. ... Bye."

***

After a long, dead-to-the-world sleep Calliope got up at two in the afternoon. She treated herself to a dark chocolate salted caramel with a room service dark roast and a Spanish omelet. Bright, faded blue heat shimmered against the windows outside complementing the desert haze over the mountains in the distance. Cars flew down dusty gray freeways next to stark concrete monoliths without their makeup on. Daytime in Paradise.

Calliope stood looking out the window watching the tourists line up for crossing lights in the choreographed dash between one massive roadside attraction and the next, clutching coupons for hot dog and Champaign buffets at noon and 3-D extravaganzas, next showing at 3:15 every day including Christmas and New Years. Hey, take a flier for full nude show downtown and a phone sex coupon too.

***

"She's coming out with a bike. ... No, a bicycle. Dressed for it too with a big 'U' on her shirt and black shorts. ... Shit, I know lieutenant; I'll do what I can. She got out too fast and I didn't get anything but her back heading out towards Las Vegas Boulevard," the short, dark woman in a business suit and low heels said into her phone.

She got up casually to leave the lobby behind Calliope, dropping the phone in her jacket pocket. When she stepped outside, she pulled out a different phone from her another pocket and tapped in a phone number.

"Yes, Carman here. She is leaving Harrah's on a bicycle and heading across the lot south towards Flamingo. 5'6", yellow and black shirt with a big red "U" on it, black bike shorts, brown ponytail, white helmet, mirror sunglasses, light blue bicycle. ... I can't do anything. ... Yes, if she uses it maybe you can find her. ... Yeah, sorry. ... I'm texting you a couple of pictures if anybody sees her. They are pretty good of her walking through the lobby. ... I'll drive around too. ... Okay, bye."

***

With most of the bags off it the bike zipped through the parking lots. Calliope turned east down Flamingo then south on Paradise to disappear into the UNLV campus. After the last evening she had decided to take no chances with whoever might be involved in this.

She wound back and forth on several campus streets and through a couple of vehicle barriers before she stopped at a campus map. The Lied Library had busy bicycle racks and a big restroom to change in. She came out with a different outfit of brown shorts and a loose white linen shirt, big sunglasses, her hair loose, and her helmet and bike clothes in her bike pannier bag. She went to find a shady bench away from the busy paths to make a few calls on her burn phone to plan her next move.

***

"Chief Daniels, there is a Ms. Dancer on your direct line. She says she was introduced by Mayor Reilly in Cleveland a few months ago," the admin said to the chief when she buzzed him at his desk.

"Uh, okay Jan, I will take it," he said looking suspiciously at the telephone. "Hello, this is Chief Daniels, Miss Dancer. You said the Mayor introduced us at my last position? What is this about?"

Calliope told the chief she had spoken with Samantha from Nationwide Professional Services and had been told to contact the chief to see if he might be able to help her find a Marlana Garcia.

84

Samantha, Sam, was Tyrone's ex. The bi-coastal office romance cooled when Tyrone did not want to leave the West for the upper Midwest and Northeast where Sam was working quickly up the Nationwide corporate ladder. She had her eye on the high-energy temptations of The Big Apple or even DC. Her high profile clients took too much ego and other kinds of stroking for Tyrone's blunter, blue-collar approach to be of much use.

Samantha contacted the chief the previous afternoon when she got a call from CEO Appleyard directly that there was a Miss Dancer in Las Vegas that should be facilitated "in an adroit and quiet manner." He sounded pissed and never contacted her unless something was up at his level. *Maybe this is a chance to score a few points, the old bastard is up to something*, she had thought to herself with a mixture of excitement and political lust.

"Call that pompous cop out there you manage and just help things along, nothing else. And stay out of it," he said and hung up.

Samantha grabbed the next plane to Las Vegas after she called Calliope to snoop, so she could "stay out of it" directly. You did not let these opportunities get by you when he was involved.

Appleyard told Calliope to call Daniels directly when she called him about the evening's excitement. "If you can't handle this yourself and I have to take my time to help you like this, then why am I paying you? And use Samantha's name with him, not mine." Calliope knew of Samantha from Tyrone's stories about her and had just hung up from her unexpected call. *This is interesting. Now he has her on it too.*

Veronica said to "watch out for him, he is dirty from back east," about Daniels when Calliope phoned her next.

"Yes Ms. Dancer, I may be able to help you with this attorney person, but I need to know more first. I will call you at your number this evening if I have time.

... Yes I have the caller ID, no wait, no read me the number dammit. ... Goodbye."

Well, I thought it was something if Samantha gave me a heads up on her. I really don't have time for this right now. I really have to get rid of them, they cost too much and always something like this, he thought after hanging up.

The Chief dialed Captain Stapleton in Homeland Security. "George, hi. Would you please email me the report from the Henderson action last night I asked you to manage for me? Also, anything you have turned up on a Calliope Dancer person who was part of it. ... Thanks, I will let you know more when it comes together."

Daniels brought Captain Stapleton with him from Cleveland as a trusted go-to person. It caused some waves, but he would do what the chief could not and had been useful in his old job before it all blew up. How Samantha ever got him moved to Las Vegas and cooled off everything he would never know, but that's what he paid for. He was working with a pushy Eric salesman from Nationwide to renegotiate his contracts and would find a way to get Samantha cheaper, or maybe into the sack. She really wanted it from him now that he was on the way up. He really should squeeze Nationwide harder now since he had built such good connections. They would squeal, but he didn't need them now, they needed him. His musings went on to becoming the next mayor of Las Vegas and maybe then replacing that old hack, Harry Reid from Searchlight, in the Senate when it came time.

He dialed up the Nevada Democratic Party Chairman to get a meeting, then went to the Mayor's office to check out the hot new admin there before his meeting with the Mayor and the little turd city manager that kept complaining about his new office costs.

"Chief, it's your wife on 06," Jan said over the phone when he picked it up. She had orders to filter all calls, his wife included. His cell had buzzed with his wife's call already and he knew she would call the office next when he put it to voice mail. *Christ, now what. I'm really getting sick of her whining.*

"Tell her I'm in a meeting and then have to go see the mayor and I'll call her when I get a chance. I'm going to the mayor's now." he said and hung up. He wore his new SWAT dress uniform today for the meeting, just to rub the City Manager's nose in it. He has squealed about paying for the new uniform design the chief wanted for homeland security operations and briefing the press. The little shit whined worse than his wife.

***

Calliope grabbed a late lunch at the UNLV cafeteria before changing back into her bike clothes and rolled off the campus. The sun fell into the hills beside her and the glitter began to come back to the city with the retreating day. She had hung out until then, waiting for Daniels to call back first. He could meet her at a coffee shop on Decauter north of downtown at 10 PM for fifteen minutes, so she had a couple of hours to kill.

The phone rang while she sat in a warm bath eating her lime crème and sipping a decent Ruby Port from the hotel bar. Veronica filled her in on more of the local gossip about the new chief and his checkered past in Cleveland. Rumor was he about to be implicated there in a grand jury bribery charge, and he and his politically social wife held lavish parties while the police force ran open loop. Even the national news had started to snoop around about it. The speculation was he made a deal with the District Attorney to resign. He got the job in Las Vegas out of the blue instead and skipped away. Nobody Veronica talked to had even guessed he was in the running for the job when the old chief retired – to spend more time with his family.

The chief's wife came from Virginia horse country and loved to have military brass from DC at her very private parties. They would show up with staff in limos to party with political movers and shakers and selected entertainment. Veronica had never been to one, but some of her colleagues had. "I have been to a couple in south Florida and know what they are, like the ones I have been to in Dubai except the guests are cheaper and more entitled," she told Cally.

Veronica's inquiries had turned up nothing about Marlana and Las Vegas was just being standard normal Las Vegas. One nasty pimp disappeared six months ago and a couple of other disappearances every now and then. The usual union organizers or low level double-crossers turned up in the proverbial shallow graves in the surrounding desert, or just didn't turn up at all. Most just moved to the next score somewhere else and never told anybody. No census kept track.

"Thanks so much, Veronica," Calliope said. "You have been a big help no matter what. I will call you when I am going to Paris next time. I promise."

She did not tell Veronica about the meeting with Daniels, but all the bits of information would be useful for dealing with him. He was a more typical inhabitant of her world, not too different from the others. She knew how to deal with his type.

***

"Past downtown my ass," Calliope said to herself walking over to the meeting. Decatur ran all the way to empty in North Las Vegas. The Wild Horse Café sat very close to the edge of the light. The glow behind her lost its grandeur this far out, and the lights of North Las Vegas looked like any other suburb at night.

The Wild Horse restaurant catered to found things. The ceiling in the dark bar had every manner of stuff hung from it. The skeletons in the upside down canoe rowed endlessly through hanging snags of tools, wheels, garden gnomes, and all manner of "interesting junk" the sign offered free drinks for. Barrels of salty peanuts stood around like islands in the thick layer of sawdust-like jetsam of discarded shells covering the floor. Carving on the smooth wooden tables and benches was encouraged to complement the found décor.

Calliope followed the overhead tide of junk into a more orderly and better lit dining room. A middle-aged man in an Armani suit with perfect bleached white hair nodded to her from a red upholstered booth. Liberace, one of the Misters of Las Vegas smiled down from his piano in a white sequined jacket with a 6-inch collar. An arresting young woman in matching money fashion and almost white, straight blond hair sat stone faced beside him. The cold, clean perfection clashed with the happy sparkles and dusty vintage.

"About time, Miss Dancer," the man said looking her up and down when she walked over. "You are ten minutes late, I was about to leave. I can only spare a few more minutes."

"Thank you for agreeing to a meeting, Chief," she said. "I am sorry to be late. It's quite a ways out here, but the taxi knew where it was," Calliope said sitting down at the end of the booth from the chief. She did not acknowledge Samantha, who likewise gave her only a mildly inquiring look in return.

"This is Samantha. She is a friend who is visiting who I believe you know. I would like her to hear what you have to say. Now, what's this all about?"

Calliope jumped right in, she had had enough false starts already to make her angry enough to skip the political game playing with the chief. *I suppose He sent her, but she has a nose for politics and anything to help her ass up the ladder. I always figured Tyrone would wise up after the sex wore off.*

"Like I told you this afternoon, Chief Daniels, I am looking for somebody, an attorney from Arizona by the name of Marlana Garcia. I have reason to believe she is here, although I can't say for sure. I went to where I heard she was last night and did not find her or any information to help me. I contacted Samantha to see if she could help and she gave me your number," Cally said nodding now to Sam.

"I know you arrived in town yesterday and were in Henderson last evening. I'm assuming that's where you went to look for this person," the chief said. Calliope kept her poker face and managed not to look surprised.

"It turned into an interesting night, as I am sure you are aware. I did not even have to give your officers a statement. Should I thank you for that?"

"I know what happens in my city," he said as irritation flickered across his features. "I really don't like these God damn SWAT jokes at all Miss Dancer. I hope you had nothing to do with it. If I find out you pulled this to help you find your missing person you will find yourself in a cell before you know it."

"I can assure you I had nothing to gain at all by exercising your police force. I don't work that way. It would have been pointless and gotten me nowhere."

"I should hope so ..."

"Wait, Steven," Samantha said, injecting herself into the conversation. "I have known Calliope for some time and can vouch for her professionalism. I would like to hear more about who Calliope is looking for and why. This could be something you need to be aware of too."

Steven disliked being interrupted and glared at Samantha. "Let's get to the point shall we. This is wasting my time."

"The point, Steve, is that there have been several murders, or at least disappearances, in various places including Europe that Ms. Garcia is connected to," Calliope said regretting her temper loosening her mouth as soon as she said it. "If you would help me locate her, I have no interest in who gets credit if it turns out she leads me to find out what's happening. I would be very happy if you got the press and I got the answers. It's a win for both of us."

Samantha's eyes gleamed for an instant. She had heard some rumblings about clients dropping off the books unexpectedly, even considering the business they were all in. *The front office really kept this one under the radar. That's why she's here and he's involved.*

"This might be very good for your career Chief Daniels," Sam said with her sweetest smile and dead eyes. "I can vouch for Ms. Dancer and Nationwide has an interest in this also. We would greatly appreciate your help in this."

Both could see wheels creak behind Daniels' face and a puffing of his chest.

Lousy poker player. "Oh yes Chief, that would be a great help to me. And thank you too Samantha," Cally said with her own saccharine coating.

"I do believe I might be able to help you ladies if this is as serious as you say. The Las Vegas Police take these matters very seriously. We always cooperate with our fellow officers wherever they might be when they need our expertise. Now Miss Dancer, is this just a police matter or have Federal agents also taken an interest? You mentioned Europe," Daniels said, waking up to opportunity.

"It is just a local police matter right now Chief. But at some point the Federal Government may be involved.

The chief dithered over if it was better for him if the Feds were already in it or if he could bring them in after he had made headway. This could be a good thing for him either way. He decided bringing in the Feds when he was ready would be another feather for his run at the Senate.

"Oh, Steve, I am excited about this. You can really move out on it," Samantha said gushing and squirming in her seat.

The chief hid his leer with no more skill than his lust to get credit for the case. "Umhum, I will get some people on this as soon as I get in the office. Might I give you a ride to your hotel Samantha?"

"Oh yes, that would be nice Steven. But maybe Calliope needs a ride too?"

Oh Christ, don't drag me into this any more. You can handle him with one sweet little claw. Fuck. "Well, I did come out here in a cab. If it would not be a huge imposition?"

Irritation flickered across the leaky Senatorial countenance. "Well, I suppose I could. It might take you a while to get a cab. I have a car."

The waiting car rolled up to the door from the edge of the Wild Horse parking lot when the chief called the bored driver. He instructed Calliope to sit in front of the silver Audi A8 limousine with black rear windows. He fondled a giggling Samantha into the back. *Wait till she gets the call to run out and handle an emergency. I am so sorry Stevie.*

"Where to Chief?" the driver said after hustling Cally into the front while holding the back door for Steve and Samantha.

"Head down to Mandalay Bay, and take surface streets.

The now animated driver hopped in ignoring Calliope and rolled out onto Decatur going south. He rolled up the tinted panel cutting off the back of the car and turned west to take quieter streets. He had practice with the chief on his nightly drives with company.

Calliope pulled a Cherry Surprise out of her purse and settled in smiling for a long drive back. *Sam will have her hands full now.*

Calliope caught the flash of white as the SUV ran the stop sign and skidded to lightly tap the back of the limo when it passed through the lonely intersection.

"Fuck!" the driver said and stopped to handle the collision.

A sickening crunch and stifled scream came from outside through the open driver's door, just before the car lurched violently as a thick bulletproof door shrieked from being torn off the back side of the car. The male screams from the rear stopped abruptly in gagging sounds and a rock of the car.

Samantha's swearing and threats were followed by a fierce, wet slapping sound, then silence.

Calliope saw nothing through the darkened privacy window and sat rigidly with a .40 caliber Sig Sauer pistol leveled into the darkness beyond her now open door where the loudest sounds came from. A dark streak smacked into the door crunching it forward on broken hinges and convulsing the wounded Audi again.

She could not fire fast enough at the blue and black shadow that flickered in front of the opening and disappeared in a fragment of a second. She emptied the clip out the door and down the empty side street, the flashing explosions blinding her and numbing her ears without her noticing. She became aware again of clutching the empty gun in a death grip with the hot slide locked back over her white hands. Slowly sight, sound, and smell expanded the tiny black tunnel she stared down turning the world back on.

"Ms. Dancer. Ms. Dancer. Put the gun down. You will not be harmed. Ms. Dancer, do you hear me?" a familiar female voice asked from outside. "You will not be harmed. Put the gun down."

Calliope's hands shook so badly she could not put another clip into the Sig. Nausea pulled her stomach down and she felt warm wetness under her on the seat. She could not lower the gun even if she wanted to.

"The gun is depleted and she is unable to reload. Her skin temperature is rising and pulse is slowing," another sibilant voice said from outside the car.

"Ms. Dancer. Do you hear me? You need to leave the car and come with me now. You will not be harmed. Do you understand Ms. Dancer?" the first voice said. "I want you to put your gun in your purse and leave the car. I will put you in another vehicle and you will be safe. Do you understand me? Get out of the car now please."

Calliope regained herself and stepped shakily out through the door opening while trying to see something outside in the dim streetlight. A hand came from beside her next to the car and took her elbow, while another gently took the forgotten gun from her. She was hustled over to a waiting car by the silent helper.

"Ms. Dancer, go with her now and you will be returned to your hotel," the first voice said to her.

"Marlana," Calliope said in a flash when her awakening mind suddenly made the connection to the voice.

Yes. I will come to your room tomorrow. Go now, I have to deal with the car," Marlana said from the other side and then she ducked inside to collect spent casings and wipe the inside down where Calliope had sat.

Cally tensed in terror again seeing for an instant gleaming blue orbs shining behind a white SUV parked behind the wrecked limo before they disappeared and the SUV settled down lower on its springs.

Now she was jerked over to the waiting car and pushed in the back seat. The vehicle sped away before she could comprehend anything else.

The driver did not speak until the car had made it to a freeway and sped towards the bright lights of Paradise.

"Calliope, your name is Calliope?"

"Yes, yes it is."

"I am taking you back to your hotel, do you understand?"

"Yes, I do. I see we are headed towards it now."

"I am going to let you off on Las Vegas Boulevard right in front. Will you be able to make it to your room?"

"Yes, I believe so," Calliope said, her mind clearing further.

The driver had turned her mirror so Calliope would not see her face. She did not want to drive up to the valet either at the hotel entrance. She would be turned loose quickly too, Cally thought.

The miasma of gratification had not changed since she had left the playground with its accompanying oblivion when Calliope was hustled out of the car. She rushed off the sidewalk through the lobby to get to her room as quickly as she could, ignoring her wet butt and shivering in the universal heat. She had not even bothered to try to see the driver or take a cell phone picture of the license plate of her

94

rescue vehicle. If Marlana did come to see her tomorrow, then she would be able to get to the bottom of things, maybe. Right now she could only focus on the safety of her room, dry clothes, hot water, and a very large handful of chocolate.

Mike Macartney

Chapter 10
San Francisco, California 1926

Sonny Gang worried about his bank and himself on his walk to dinner down Washington Street from the bank to the Sam Wo restaurant. The 1920s had not been kind to the Canton Bank of San Francisco. The McKean Mining client coming from Sacramento would ask questions. The last bits of Nevada gold no longer covered the loans to the Hop Sing Tong and they kept pushing him to funnel more to their Wo Hop To Tong brothers in Wanchai. There were too many hands out, and the bank was starting to get shaky. He worried the next time the dogs barked it would be him they left on the floor full of bullets.

Early on the Nevada gold money came easy from the Chinese immigrants in Virginia City, Tuscarora, and Gold Hill. The Canton Bank of San Francisco helped them send money back to China and became wealthy like their Caucasian brothers at Crocker, Wells Fargo, and Bank of California. But, as the Comstock petered out with the other strikes there were only blips now. The boom of the 1920s floated the banks on the other side of town higher while Canton Bank sank lower. The anti-immigrant Chinese Exclusion Act of 1882 had been extended even further in 1924. Mistrust of institutions by the penned up Chinese communities hardened, even for a Chinese bank like the Canton. Triads and fighting tongs kept their traditional place in the new land's communities as handmaidens to poverty, mistrust, and corruption as they had in the old lands too. Sonny kept juggling his many masters, and the bank kept sinking.

Changming "Tommy" Tong had come to meet Sonny because the money he invested with the bank from his clients in California and Nevada never seemed to grow like it should. The money that he sent to Shanghai even seemed to be shrinking by the time it got there. Wells Fargo went up and Canton Bank went down. Tommy could not put all his client's money in Wells Fargo, or he would. His clients were Chinese and did not trust banks and Caucasian banks did not trust them either, nor were the clients prepared to send their money directly to China either.

Sam Wo's had a crowd as usual, but Sonny could always get a table when he needed one. He drank whiskey while he waited for Tommy and worried some more.

Sonny's heart sank further when he saw Tommy come in and ask the waiter for him. The waiter waved his hand towards Sonny and the wiry, sunburned little man came up and bowed to him at his table. A brown low class laborer would never comprehend the financial world Sonny lived in, he thought. *Aiie, he probably counts on his fingers. How will I be able to explain it to him so his simple mind will be able to grasp it?*

"Good evening Mr. Gang. It was very good of you to meet with me," Tommy said in stiff Mandarin. Sonny would have to speak in Mandarin also, not his native Cantonese. Tommy most likely spoke Shanghainese Sonny figured, and his Mandarin was as limited as Tommy's. *Even worse*, he thought standing to bow to Tommy.

"I hope you were able to find the restaurant easily Mr. Tong," Sonny said. "San Francisco streets are always a problem for people from out of town."

"Thank you, I was able to ride your wonderful cable car right from the ferry to Chinatown." Sonny sat down not waiting for his guest and contemplated how to get through the rest of the meeting as quickly as possible.

"Please sit Mr. Tong and have something to eat. I have ordered food and the very good plum wine they have here. I hope it is acceptable to you?" Sonny said pouring tea for Tommy and then himself. The alcohol began to relax him.

"Yes, thank you Mr. Gang. I have traveled a long way and have not had time to eat since this morning in Oakland."

"Now what may I do for you?" Sonny asked after they had time to sip the tea and each had a cup of wine set before them.

"As you know, I have people from Nevada and California who use the Canton Bank to deposit their money and send it to their families in China. They have asked me to come to see you because they are concerned it has become more difficult to do this now. It is taking a very long time. Some have heard from family that less money than they sent came to them."

"Mr. Tong, you must understand that it is very difficult to send money to China. The Canton bank is very well respected in China, but some people there do not trust banks and they are far away from Canton. The bank takes special actions to see they are told, but people that work with the bank to do this cost money for their efforts so there is a little less money for the family. It is called an expense," Sonny said nodding with pursed lips. "Banking is very complicated and there are many costs involved to protect your money for you. That may be difficult for you to understand at first. There are complicated numbers to be accounted for, and I am certain that you would understand even if I could show them to you. They are only kept at the bank and only the most senior people can understand them. I do not even know them all. I assure you that I am very serious in taking care of your money and making very sure you always get the very best deal with it."

Tommy looked bewildered. "Oh I understand. Nevertheless, I need to always be very sure my peoples' money is protected. It is that some of them have heard stories from their relatives about less money from the bank too. They did not make what they hoped for at the bank here. I am sorry to take your time away from your job, but I must ask. What can I say to calm down my clients?" he said.

Sonny leaned back in his chair and almost smiled as the waiter interrupted to begin putting plates of food on the table with more wine. Sonny gulped his down and asked for another cup, while Tommy barely touched his.

"Tommy, you need to tell them that banking is a difficult and very complicated thing. You need to say that you met with the senior man who is taking care of their money and he is very concerned with protecting it for them. He is doing all he can and hiring only the best and most trustworthy people in China, personally, to get the money to the families. Tell them he is very confident of these people, but he checked to make sure they are doing all the right things just to be sure. It may cost a little extra money, but you understand that, Sonny. Just make sure they do too. They understand how China is. They have to do this themselves all the time. They know how things work there."

"Okay, yes, I think I understand now," Tommy said with a sad look. "I will just have to explain how it is and what you are doing for them. I am sorry I had to take up your time like this, but you understand. My clients were worried."

"I understand, explaining things to uneducated people who do not understand the modern world is hard. I am glad we understand each other and now you can appreciate how complicated things are. It is good that you came to explain this concern to me. Now I can ensure you get the best deal and nobody is cheating you or your clients. I will look into it personally and make corrections if I find anything."

Tommy ate quickly and self consciously before thanking Sonny again and excusing himself to go to his room for the evening. He asked Sonny for directions to Western Union so he could telegraph his clients and let them know how well his meeting with the senior man at the bank had gone, before bowing profusely to Sonny and merging into the evening hustle of Chinatown in the street outside.

Sonny was relieved. It had been easier than he had expected to impress this peasant. He ordered a glass of whiskey with a smile to celebrate before heading to a gambling house. He was sure it would be a lucky night.

***

Sonny had just sat down heavily in his tiny office when the bank manager himself stormed in and slammed the door behind him. He began shrieking at once about, "What had Sonny done! You are a fool! Do you know what this means? Even Chu Li Chan himself came to see me to say The Six Companies were very concerned about the bank!"

"Wait, sir, but, oh, oh I do not understand," Sonny stammered. "What are you saying? Please sir."

"You, you, your accounts have left the bank, aiie, we are ruined."

"What? My accounts? I have not heard anything sir."

"McKean Mining pulled all their deposits, and demanded their silver and gold from our vaults. Others from Nevada and California have too. Karl Phillips himself handles McKean and has taken the claims of all associated parties under his firm's representation through their agent Changming Li Tong. The bullion is not there! Three-million, two-hundred-eighty-thousand dollars is missing from their holdings. Tong had Phillips stop all transactions and demand we audit everything his clients have deposited in Canton. Everything. You, you, you have destroyed the bank!"

The manager flung open the door and ordered two uniformed bank guards standing outside to keep Sonny locked in his office until the police came. He sputtered a stream of unintelligible words at Sonny and hurried away as one of the guards came into Sonny's office and closed the door to wait.

Sonny held his white face in his trembling hands and tried to breathe.

***

```
Mr. Zhizhu Song
McKean Mining and Tool
601 P Street
Sacramento, California

May 11, 1926

Phillips settlement. Recovered  82
percent. Deposited Crocker Bank, San
Francisco.
Now Shanghai Commercial Bank in China.
Move Hong Kong soon. Chang and crime
syndicates now war with Communists.
Sonny Tong suicide by hanging San
Francisco jail.

Changming Tong
STOP
```

Chapter 11

Las Vegas, Nevada Monday July 21, 2014

Bells rang in Calliope's dreams. She came awake disoriented, slowly remembering that the unnatural sound came from a rarely used telephone on the nightstand between the beds.

"Hello," she said managing to pick up the receiver before the ringing stopped.

"Ms. Dancer, I will be waiting at the second floor Starbucks at 11:45. I will see you then," Marlana's voice said before she hung up.

The faded red numbers on the clock radio in the darkness said 10:18. She staggered over to the thick blackout drapes peering through a crack into the burning morning light outside before stiffly careening in the general direction of the bathroom.

Calliope perked up to almost cheerful after a shower and a lemon whip special to wake up and clear her head. The bizarre events of the evening had jarred investigation off dead center in her mind. It was very clear after last night that Marlana was definitely involved in all of it, she thought getting dressed. *She is more dangerous than I imagined. What a terrifying crash, or whatever the hell it was. I don't know what Tyrone will do now with Samantha gone now too. They are way too powerful to be killed like that. A police chief too, right in the middle of the city. This is more than I imagined.*

The morning shows on TV had finished when Calliope turned on the big TV on the dresser to see if she could find out something more about what had happened the night before. Stories from the local press about the missing Las Vegas police chief crawled demandingly across the bottom of the Perry Mason rerun. She looked on her phone for more. The police chief's damaged and burned car had been discovered in an industrial section of North Las Vegas, but the police refused to say anything else to the swarming press pool. The news clips lacked any real information. They showed repetitive videos from behind barricades of a blackened wreck sitting in the middle of an intersection with blue suited investigators swarming it.

Cally tramped out of the elevator to find the Starbucks to get the taste of room coffee and the night before out of her mouth. A young woman with coffee dressed in jeans, sunglasses, and an LA Dodgers tee shirt walked up behind her when she turned away from the order station with her coffee. Marlana asked Calliope to walk with her outside to the pool and said nothing else. They got a table at the far end of the pool away from most of the litter of bodies consuming alcohol and laying under the great white star overhead.

"You are persistent Ms. Dancer. Annoying." Marlana said when they sat down.

"And, you are a mystery to me Ms. Garcia."

"Possibly. But, you seem to have not let it frustrate you."

"Okay enough of this," Calliope said unable to keep up the charade. "It looks like you had no difficulty finding me, and whatever happened last night, well it was more than you just driving by la-de-da. You do know who was in the car with me don't you?"

"Yes, a strange creature, an unusual person from what I saw of her. Broken and disgusting."

"No, what? You saw her that way? Do you have any idea what you saw?"

"Yes Ms. Dancer I do. More than you might know. You make your living off that, I don't."

Calliope blinked and stopped. She did not wish to get dragged any farther along by the woman across from her by her own big mouth. She had tried being direct to extract more from her and instead had been surprised by what she, or they, already knew about her and her business. Her usual control of people and events collapsed leaving her confused and at a dead end, like so much else in this case.

Tyrone and Appleyard were their own kind of dangerous, but ever since she had been a little girl her great aunt and uncle had taught her how to recognize them and others like them. She had managed that ability to her own ends, especially with the help of Hermione's candy. Her rich and powerful clients rubbed shoulders with the other side in their own unique ways, but they usually did not see what Calliope did. They sought her out for her ability to see and manage the wispy boundaries between their worlds and the alternate ones swirling all around. Smoothing interfaces from one reality to another made it a very lucrative practice. Then Marlana and whoever else she worked for came along and turned it all over.

"You really should not meddle Ms. Dancer. Go back and tell your client you have been unable to find out anything. It would be better that way," Marlana said, leaning forward over her coffee.

"No, I can't do that Ms. Garcia. It's too far along for that," Cally said before she could stop herself. *Damn! Damn my big mouth.*

Marlana sat for a moment staring blankly at Calliope, thinking.

"I am not sure what to do with you yet. You could be useful, or you could be a threat. You know you could disappear here and never be heard of again?"

Cold shivers ran down Calliope's body. She felt her hair stand up and her ears tingle at such a lack of emotion in the threat. She knew the cold violence behind some of her clients, like Appleyard, but this was different. She knew her very existence was being considered, her continued life being judged for some value she did not understand at all. Genuine fear seldom visited her, but this was one of those times. It came from a cold, quiet young woman in a baseball cap sitting across from her holding her life in her hands.

Cally's mind jerked to flee, she wanted to jump up wildly, scream, attract attention, stop the danger, and could not. Her head shrieked at her that no matter what she did, if she was judged a threat by this woman she would be simply killed right here and now, or somewhere else with neither malice nor anger. No escape existed anywhere. She knew the stone faced woman across from her sat weighing her life's value, and the best way to snuff her breath at the same time for getting too close to this.

Finally she spoke.

"I am going to show you something. You will have to decide which side you are on then. Come with me," Marlana said. She stood up looked down at Calliope with the unchanging blank face.

Not believing her quivering legs could hold, Calliope stood and followed Marlana out of the Starbucks while a tall, straight woman whom she had not noticed sitting in the back corner of the coffee bar glided in smoothly a few steps behind them.

Song

Mike Macartney

Chapter 12

The bitter cold late fall wind smacking Lee in the face made his ears ache. Fading blue-gray light of a sun already below the horizon brought frost to rocks still cold from the night before. A rare muggy day for the desert chilled into a haze of moisture in the gloom of the November air. Lee would be happy to get back to his hard room in Silver Peak to warm up by the stove. Tramping over the sand and around the sagebrush and dry rabbit grass across the sprawling alluvial fans spreading out from the hills had yielded few useful stones. The trough between the hills would lead him back to town, to a warm room and food.

He entertained himself with daydreams sloughing through the twilight of how to beat the new roulette wheel he had built for the Silver Queen. They brought the wheel overland by stagecoach, all the way from Will & Fink in San Francisco. Lee Toy had built the table and the betting layout for them. He had also built the big Wheel-of-Fortune they had, but he rarely played it. The big wheel was very hard to beat. You needed special luck.

What is that, Lee thought coming back from his dreaming and stopping abruptly. *Sparkling blue dots in the black shadows.* The hair stood up on the back of his neck as shivers went over his shoulders and down the backs of his arms.

Must be turquoise there? Huh, it's like a face! What, did Indians make it? They scrape the brown rocks to make their magic pictures, but no blue eyes.

"Hello there Indian face!" *Ahh, my stomach feels better now, just a big rock with turquoise that looks like the lion mask with six blue eyes.* "Hello there lion."

"Aiee. The hiss. The wind is talking to me. Wind, stop that! The lion will not like you playing with Lee.

"Wind, stop that!"

"Ahhhh! Lion stop that! I can see you there in the dark." *My legs are shaking and my chest, hard to breathe. It's big, no not a lion. What? Black. Many legs and face with blue eyes. Just, so still. Yes, yes a big rock. The eyes do not move. Ha, it's only a big rock in the shadow,* Lee thought relaxing now as he began to walk again with a smile about how silly he was, only the wind.

"Ahhhh! Lion stop that! I can see you there in the dark. Huhhhhssss, huhhhhssss, huhhhhssss."

"No! No! Stop! Stop! Do not mock me! *Why is lion doing this? Think! Think! Why is lion doing this? Just rocks talking. Why is this?* Lee froze again leaning to stare desperately into the violet dimness.

"No! No! Stop! Stop! Huhhhhssss, huhhhhssss, huhhhhssss. Do not mock me! Huhhhhssss, huhhhhssss, huhhhhssss."

Think! Think! Why does lion make fun of me? Breathe slower. Think. Breathe.

"Lion, what are doing? Are you making fun of me?"

"Lion, what are you doing? Are you making fun of me?"

"Lion!" *Oh, wait maybe lion doesn't know what I am saying to him. It was very, very hard to come to San Francisco and not be able to speak to Americans. They talked loudly and pointed, and got mad at me for not talking back. I could not say anything to them. So hard. Still hard. They still make fun of the way I talk.*

"Lion!"

"Wait lion. 'Lee Toy.' I am Lee Toy. My name is Lee Toy. Lee Toy. Lee Toy."

"Lee Toy."

"Ha-ha, Yes! I am Lee Toy."

"Lee Toy."

Yes, that's it. Lion speaks like a lion. He understands Chinese. He's a lion. No! No he is a spider! Ohhhh, he is a big spider!

"Huhhhhssss, huhhhhssss, huhhhhssss."

Aiee, breathe, breathe. "Lion, Sp-pider. Lee Toy will not hurt you. Lee Toy is a man. Lee Toy is your friend."

"Lee Toy man. Lion Sp-pider."

"Lee Toy man. Lee Toy man."

"Lee Toy man."

"You, you spider. You spider."

"Lee Toy man. You spider. You Song. Song Tklat. Lee Toy man. Song Tklat."

"Ahhhh. Song. Song. Yes, yes My name is Lee Toy. Your name is Song? My name is Lee Toy. Your name is Song. Yes. Yes."

"My name is Song. Your name is Lee Toy. Yes. Yes."

A spider in the morning is good luck. A terrible spider in this American land at night, so big. Big good luck? Maybe big good luck? Lee thought shaking from the cold and the fear.

"Spider, Song. I, Lee Toy, must go. I am very cold now. Dark. I will come back. I will look for you tomorrow." *Back up slowly. Walk. Wave. Walk faster. Keep walking. Keep walking.* "Lee Toy will come back." *Keep walking.*

"Ahuhh, cannot see the rocks in the dark now. No, he is gone now. No more blue eyes in the shadow now. Spider is gone. No sound, just wind. Must to get back quickly. I am very cold now. Walk fast, Lee thought, stumbling rapidly forward, then running towards the town below convincing himself that it had all been his imagination and would only be rocks in the light of day.

***

It's hot in here. No miners here tonight. The new roulette wheel is covered and nobody is even playing poker. No luck tonight.

"Hello Lee. Sorry, no gambling tonight. Do you want a drink?" The bartender stood behind Lee as he stared into the gaming room at the Silver Queen.

"Hello, David. I sorry new roulette table not working. I going be lucky tonight."

"Yeah. That's always what you say, Lee. Everybody likes the big six wheel you made. They all like those Chinaman animals you put on it. Some of 'em worry it'll spell them and why I have a *Chinaman thing like that*. But, it just makes everybody talk about it and want to beat it. You did a good job of it."

"Thank you David. I happy you like. Can I have some your peanuts and water please?

"You need more than that to eat. Stop the worrying 'bout how much money you got to gamble with. You need to take better care of yourself. Eat better."

"I had food today. I feel good. I out looking for stones to build things with. It cold wind all day. Is good to come here get warm."

"You find any gold out there? I know what you go out there for." David said smiling. He liked Lee, even if he was a Chinaman.

"Ha-ha, no I did not find the gold today." *But, I did find luck, maybe. Nowhere to try it tonight though. I wonder now if it was even real. Maybe I should eat more.*"

"You don't look so good Lee. Why don't you eat something? You can afford it."

"Okay David. I hungry walked much today. I buy your special tonight?"

Might as well get something out of him. No business tonight and peanuts and water costs me too, the bartender thought.

***

The next day dawned clear and still under a faded blue sky with feathery cloud streaks.

It's not like Shanghai, Lee thought walking up from the yellow pine buildings next to the hills he had come to at the start of the 20th century in America. *Shanghai is old and wet in the winter and hot and wet in the summer. The dry cold is not so bad here with the warm sun and the heat in the summer is only bad in the daytime, not all night too. It's so empty and hard though. No trees, no water, no civilization here. The Americans do not like us Chinese here either, but not as bad as California. At least here I can own land and can pass it to my sons.*

Here is the place from last night. The wash in the side of the hill is not so dark now. Hum, it seems bigger, but the sand and gravel is broken on top and has holes pushed down in it. I see where the spider was. What if he's down around the curve? Is he waiting for me to walk down into his giant web to grab me? Should I go down there? I'll climb up on the hill to see if his web is there.

No web and no spider greeted Lee ahead and gradually he relaxed again and went about his work searching the ground for precious stones and maybe gold.

The wind is making my ears ache. No lucky spider today. I need to work on the bar shelves for Mr. Parker. He wants it done soon. No time to make it with anything fancy for him. He said he will not pay and just wants shelves for his bottles. 'Just make somethin' simple and cheap where the mirror was. No 'spensive stuff now. I know how you Chinamen want to run up the bill. I won't pay for that.' Ahh, here is something I can use. Quartz."

***

"Hello, Lee Toy. How are you this fine, soft summer evening?"

"Aiee Spider! How are you so quiet behind me? You always come up that way."

"I *am* that way."

"You always say things like that, and never tell me what *that* means. I have told you of myself and Shanghai and San Francisco and the Triads I paid to come to America. You never tell me about how you came here."

"You have taught me a great deal about your world. I thank you for the two languages you have given me, all the stories of your travels, and the things you have shown that me you make for the people who think of you as just a Chinaman, one of those foreigners who only wants their jobs and their money. Why do you tell me all those things?"

"Because Spider, you listen to me. You try to understand me. You do not judge me. You learn so fast, and you always to thank me. You have become my friend."

"Thank you Lee Toy. I have a difficult time understanding what you mean by 'judge,' or how it feels to you. Your happy, and sad, and afraid are difficult for me to understand. But, I still think you trying to tell me something else."

"You say funny things. I don't know how to explain them to you. You listen to me, and it makes me feel good. But you say you do not understand what it means. Yet you have so many words and you seem to care about what I say. Is it just words to you?"

"Yes, it is the words to me, Lee Toy. It is what they mean and what you tell me with the words. How they fit together to explain you and me here in this world. I am not human. I cannot know what it means to be human. Maybe I will someday, but I have only been here a short while."

"That makes me sad. I thought you liked me and understood me. I thought you were my friend."

"I hear what you are telling me. I know our relationship matters to you and also I do not know what those words mean to you exactly. They are only approximations of what is in your mind after all."

"You think strangely. But you said you understood friendship? Doesn't it mean something to you?"

"If I say yes, that is it, then you may think a different thing than I mean. I could say I understand what you feel, but that would not be true. I can tell you I place value on friendship, an importance. Is that what you mean by feel?"

"Nevertheless, Spider, you have told me you know what loyal and honor and true means. You said you had a friend before and that you knew what it was."

"You make many things. Things that are difficult and that your people think are beautiful and have value, yes?" the spider said changing the subject.

"Yes. I do love to make things and some of them are very special and it is hard for me to part with them to people who do not seem to care as much. But I have to make a living," Lee said with a tinge of sadness.

"Where do you get the ideas from for what you make?"

"That's hard to explain. It just happens and I have an idea for something somebody wants and I create it."

"So you create it from what you think it should look like in your mind and what it should do?"

"Yes. That's part of it. It also has to be created from what I feel too. That's what makes the best things."

"Do you use special tools for what you make?"

"Yes, of course. You have to have good tools to make beautiful things. But more than that, you have to know how to use those tools in the right way to construct what you wish to create."

"Do you, I do not know the right word, is it *respect* the tools? Are they as important as the things you make? Do you make the tools to make the things you create too?"

"Yes, respect, but you must feel your tools too. Every tool is different, even the same kind of tool as another, like a paintbrush or a chisel. Each one is unique, and you have to sense it and touch it from inside yourself so it is connected to your work to make the best things with it."

"Would you say that your tools are loyal to you and are your friends?"

"Hum, I never thought of it like that. That's interesting to think about. Tools are not alive, but my feeling when I use them makes them work better, and the old ones I have had for a long time feel special. They

115

have a life in them that is different from the new ones. They are comfortable, and I miss them when they break or wear out, but *friends*, I don't know if that is it. Friends are more than that."

"That is the hard part for me to understand. The *more than*. I'm sorry that I don't understand all of what you are telling me, but I think *sorry* means something like feeling to you. Not just that I don't understand and wish I did. But, I do understand what loyalty is and I am always loyal to makers. I know that my loyalty extends to you for what you have done for me and taught me. Do you understand, Lee Toy?"

"Yes Spider. It is part of being a friend and I know that you do not understand why it is. I'm not sad as much, because you really don't know. It's just the way you are."

"You help me. I do not forget that. But I am confused by it also. I have to think about it. I do want us to be friends.

"Ha-ha, yes Spider. You're very confusing too!"

***

"Good evening Spider. I hope your day was a good one."

"Hello, it is nice to see you again Lee Toy. You know when I come now it seems."

"Oh yes, or you make noise to help, maybe?"

"Who can say, I may be more clumsy."

"I brought you something to show you. Something I've made. I hope you like it."

"Yes. It's beautiful.

"Look inside."

"Yes, yes. The stars are very beautiful. The hills and the valleys, you have captured them without showing them. How did you do it? I'm amazed. You have created them so well and so simply."

"Thank you so much. It has been a difficult and exciting box to make. I traded much other work and walked many miles to find everything. I'm so happy you like it. You're always talking about the stars and I wanted to capture them in the box."

"I see it. You have made the great road of stars real in a box. It is quite remarkable. Is that what I look like? On the top of the box?"

"Yes it is. I made that part as real as I could. You do not know what you look like? How can that be?"

"I can't see myself. My eyes look forward and only my front legs can reach them and hold things in front of them for me to see. I've seen reflections of my self now-and-then, but that is not like seeing myself in a way others do in their minds."

"Now you can see yourself. It's good that my simple skill has helped you do that. It makes my work even better for me. Now, I must also tell you sadder news."

"What is that?"

"I am leaving Silver Peak."

"Oh, I will miss our talks in the evening. Where will you go?"

"I hear there is gold and jobs in Tonopah. There are many Chinese going there, and I miss my people."

"I understand what you are saying. Where is Tonopah?"

"It's very close to here, only about 30 miles to the north. You could walk there in a day."

"Are there many people there? I must be careful still."

"Yes, but there are still places near where people seldom go."

"It could be dangerous for me. I avoid people when I can. They are looking for gold all over and go all over."

"You did not avoid me."

"No I did not. I was ready to meet the people here finally. It is a very good thing to have met you first.

"It is already three years into the new century in America, and it's the New Year in China. It is an auspicious time to make a journey and to begin new things. I must do what I came to this country for.

"If you come to the hills to the east of Tonopah high up, I will come there and look for you there. I would like to have you as my friend still. But I have to go to where I can make money and where more Chinese are. I hope you understand."

"Okay, I will figure out how. You are correct, it's time for me to go further than here also."

***

"Is hard for you here? You do not talk as much. Your mind is somewhere else," Song said to Lee.

"They do not like the Chinese here at all. They think we work too hard and have come to take their work away from them. The miners made a union to stop us from working, and when we complain they tell us the law says we cannot speak against the white people because we are Chinese. We can own land, but they only want us to wash their clothes for money to buy it with. It's like Shanghai where the emperor's civil servants wanted to tell us what we must do and took our money whenever they wished for themselves. That's why I left Shanghai."

"You should leave and go somewhere else. Can you do that?"

"California is worse. We can wash clothes or be a slave building railroads, but they will not even let us own land. Just like Shanghai."

"It's winter soon, and then another year. Maybe it will help and the people who do not like you will not be as bad then."

"Oh, Spider where do you come from? It is the same in China. Only if you have gold and wealth is it better. If you don't others tell you what you should do and not do, and you have to work for them."

"It's not efficient. Is wealth, gold, how you become happy?"

"Yes it is. When you are wealthy you are happy, and can find a wife, and the miners work for you then. You can pay the civil servants to do what you want. It's good luck and that makes you happy."

"I am sorry. That's very hard for me to understand."

"I am tired tonight. We will have to talk about this another time," Lee said sadly.

***

The lights are bright tonight all over. Something is happening. I wonder if Lee Toy is all right.

Lee Toy? No, he moves differently. Different temperature signature. Cooler. Jerking and stumbling. Smaller. The other behind him is much stronger and quicker. Hotter. Primitive kill. Not efficient. Is he dangerous? Everything active. I could destroy him in an instant before he could move one step. No. Too much risk. No imminent threat. He has left the person he attacked dead and cooling, and he runs away without seeing me. Clumsy and inefficient. Just let him go.

Others came to discover the body of the dead man. The spider's sensitive ears heard them talking about the fighting with the Chinamen and "this would not help," in the English language Lee Toy had taught him. It was harder to understand, because Lee would always speak Chinese, but he would learn it quickly.

The spider did not see Lee after that. The spider waited patiently until the short cold days for him to return, he was a maker, even if he was an alien creature.

After the coldest time when the days grew longer again Lee came back. The spider had gone back to the place where he had first met Lee and now watched him came up the hill. Lee had been looking for his friend too.

Song had waited for Lee to show him what he had found for him. He handed him a large reddish stone with streaks of white and yellow in it. Lee smiled and became excited. They talked about what would have to be done and where Song had broken the stone out of the bedrock around it, but no one could know about him or how it was found. They would need others to help them mine the gold and build a mining company to keep it – and the real prospector secret.

119

Mike Macartney

Chapter 13
New York City, New York 1996

Carmine's uncle Anthony sent him to university after his father Joseph was shot in 1963 stepping out of their house in Queens. Tony and Joe had been inseparable as children growing up in the Little Italy section of East Harlem. Their father Arturo, Carmine's grandfather, had come from Calabria in 1927 and settled with them and their sisters Maria and Adrianna on 109ᵗʰ street in New York. Their mother, Carlotta, died in 1928 from blood poisoning and Arturo raised them all by himself working as a butcher. He never remarried, even though many of the single women in the neighborhood brought him food and talked to him when they had the chance for a time after Carlotta passed.

The boys drifted into the Ndrangheta crime syndicate and eventually became soldiers in the Lucchese Family. Arturo loved his children, but never could talk them out of becoming Mafiosi. The struggle of a sometimes employed butcher in the early 20th century New York Italian ghetto was not the career path either of the boys chose. Maria married a plumber with a good job, but Adrianna never could find a decent man, or any man at all. She lived with her father until his heart attack in 1949 and then took care of him until he passed in 1951. She kept the rent controlled apartment for the rest of her life. She rented a room to a woman named Cecelia who lived there with her until Adrianna passed in 2006 when she was 94. Cecelia was only 92 at the time, but passed within 6 months while fighting to keep the apartment.

Tony moved in with Joe's wife Candy and his nephew Carmine after Joe contracted lead poisoning.

Five years later he paid for Carmine to start college at CUNY. He wanted to be a lawyer. Tony figured he could always use another good lawyer and anyway the kid was smart but would never be a decent soldier. He ever said very much about what he wanted at all, he was very quiet. He would go into his room whenever Tony or Candy had people over and only ever came out when Candy's cousin Frank visited from out west. He never spoke much about why he came to New York or what he actually did for a living to Carmine's family, but Frank and Carmine hit it off and would go off in a corner and talk and talk.

Carmine went straight through City University to a JD and passed the New York Bar on his first try. He never did become the kind of mouthpiece Uncle Tony wanted him to be, and instead went to Wall Street to start as an associate at one of the old silk stocking firms in Manhattan.

Tony and Candy finally got tired of the life and left Queens in 1979 for a planned development in Coral Springs, Florida.

***

"Carmine, would you take this call for Mr. Hamilton?" Joan said when Carmine picked up the phone.

"Hello, this is Carmine Salvatore. Mr. Hamilton asked that I speak with you," Carmine said when the call transferred.

"Yes, hello. I call Mr. Hamilton directly. Who are you," the accented voice said.

"I am Carmine Salvatore, senior associate for Mr. Hamilton. He is tied up in court today. He asked me to speak with you. What can I do for you?"

"Well, if Mr. Hamilton busy today I call another firm. I have no time wait. Next year Hong Kong become China again. Need to do things before."

"I am positive that we can help you, Mr. ... ? If you would like to tell me what your issue is then I will make sure that the right people at Hamilton are available for you. As I said Mr. Hamilton is in court this

122

morning and I have his full authority and confidence to assist you. I will brief him personally when he returns.

"Yes, you get Mr. Hamilton for me?"

"I'm sorry. I meant the firm, Hamilton, Smith, and Baker. Mr. Hamilton is not available. I will be delighted to take as much time as you need to explain what your needs are. And, if I cannot assist you I will personally refer you to a firm that will. If you would like to have a referral, I will do that right now, but if you want to tell me a little bit about your needs I will make sure you are taken care of."

Mr. Hamilton was sitting in his office talking to one of his old clients about his new building plans for his home on Long Island. He took few new clients himself, and when one called out of the blue that even Joan had difficulty understanding, he passed the call off to Carmine to deal with.

"I do not want to talk on telephone. I will be in New York in two week. I can meet you?"

"Yes, Mr. ... I will be happy to meet with you at the end of the month when you come to New York. How about the 28th? Is that okay for you?

"Yes, I be there 28 May in New York."

"Would you please tell me a little something of what we would be meeting about? In that way I'll have some time to get ready so I will not waste your time at the meeting, Mr. – your name? I do not believe I caught it when Mr. Hamilton transferred your call to me."

"Oh, yes. My name is Chen. I looking for attorney to help company business in America. Need too for business in South America. My bank tell me call Mr. Hamilton."

"Okay, that should be fine. I will wait to meet you to discuss your business. Can you tell us who referred you at your bank? I know lots of bankers."

"Mr. Bao-jin Zhang at Wells Fargo give me telephone number Mr. Hamilton. He say call him direct. I wish tell business to you when meet."

"Then, Mr. Chen, I will wait until we meet to find out about your business. Is there a way I can contact you to confirm the meeting? Do you know where our offices are?"

"I give you email how to call me. Please, what is email I send to?"

"My email is S-dot-S-A-L-V-A-T-O-R-E-at-H-S-B-L-A-W-dot-C-O-M. My phone number is 212-555-9000 extension-8. I will send you all the information about the meeting. I will look forward to seeing you on May 28ᵗʰ at our offices in Manhattan. I will send you all the details to confirm in an email when I get yours."

Carmine hung up the phone shaking his head. It would probably be a waste of time in any case. But he did have Hamilton's direct line, so maybe he would show up with something. He thought better of it when he looked up Bao-Jin Zhang and he turned out to be the director of the Hong Kong branch of Wells Fargo Bank.

***

The subway ride had been muggy, crowded, and smelly coming to work. The mayor was cracking down on graffiti and the cars were cleaner now at least. Carmine checked his to-do for the day and saw he had the meeting with the Chinese businessman today. He had been busy with two long term clients doing leveraged buy outs to cash out their companies and retire. He figured Chen wanted to get money out of Asia with the market collapse spreading there. He would hear the details when they met and could hand him off to the firm's Asia market lead if he needed to. They had tons of old clients in the US and the UK to keep them busy and did not have much more than a token practice with Asia.

Carmine grabbed coffee and chatted up Joan to see what David might have going for him in case he had to juggle the day and drop something on him. He went to stare at the pile of pink message slips already piling up on his cluttered desk. He couldn't do much with the phone already ringing when he walked in.

He spent the morning talking to Chase Manhattan bankers about stock pricing on the Carlsen buyout and then dragged Paul Arthur into his office to find out what the plan was for closing which divisions, and which employees would be moved or let go at what price. Many were old time employees working on obsolete product lines from when Carlsen first built the business. The banks had to have the plan and the numbers before they would price their investment and were screaming because the plan was late and Daniel Carlsen still wanted control. Carmine feared it would blow up the deal unless they got him a plan he could accept for his people and his pet projects that were both past their prime.

Three o'clock rolled around and Carmine had not even answered the intercom page from Carla. She said, "Carmine your three o'clock is here" loudly for the second time to him in person. Her frustration showed from being dragged away from her own work to get all the letters out and the SEC filings organized for two deals at the same time.

"Oh shit," Carmine said. "Thanks, tell him to wait a minute and I will come out and get him." He pushed some of the piles into a less precarious structure and turned over the top pages on them, before giving up on making any kind of neat space on the opposite side of his desk for his visitor. Both guest chairs were stacked with paper. He moved the pile of one onto the floor in the corner before dashing out to the lobby.

Both Mr. Chen and a young, freckled blond woman with her hair tied back looked up at him when he slowed to a walk, entering the lobby in a more dignified manner. Carmine took in the expensive Italian suit and stern face in a glance. The woman had a dark face from the sun and hard lines around her quiet eyes and mouth.

"Mr. Chen. It's nice to meet you," Carmine said walking up with an outstretched hand. "I hope my directions made us easy to find."

"Hello, Mr. Salvatore," Chen said standing to shake hands while smiling with his mouth. "I have brought Miss Carter. My English not good sometimes. She help me. She understand business and I trust her."

"To be clear, is Miss Carter part of your business and I can discuss confidential information with both of you?"

"Yes, she is and can hear all. She can sometimes speak for business too. I hope this okay for you? ."

"Why of course. Just making sure. Then I do not mind at all," Carmine said smiling at the woman. "Thank you for coming Miss Carter. Please wait here just a moment while I check to see if our room is available."

Carmine walked over to the lobby receptionist to ask about a conference room now that there were three people. After a little wrangling he got Alan Baker's private conference room since he was only in the office a few days a month now. The gossip was the other partners were fighting with him about his buyout and it was not going smoothly. He locked up his office and conference room and left his abrasive admin outside to keep everybody else out. Carmine had always been nice to Carla and it only cost him dinner on the firm's tab to get use of the room.

"Thank you, Carla," he said with a big smile when the three came up to her desk to get the key. "I owe you."

"Yes, Carmine, you do. Don't let this get around."

"I won't, don't worry."

"Now, does anybody want water before we get started?" Carmine asked Chen and his companion when they sat down in the soft red leather chairs around the George Nakashima redwood table.

"Yes, a little water please." the translator said for both after looking at Mr. Chen who nodded.

Carmine poured three glasses from the carafe on the table while Mr. Chen set his briefcase in front of himself and waited to begin.

"Now Mr. Chen," Carmine said look at him. "What can we do for you?"

"Mr. Salvatore, thank you for seeing us," Miss Carter began. "Mr. Chen asked me to explain some of why we are here for him. As you are aware there is a financial collapse in South Asia taking place. It is spreading to Hong Kong, and Hong Kong lease expires and it will be returned to the People's Republic of China next year in 1997. Mr. Chen represents several interests in Hong Kong, Shanghai, and the United States also who wish to protect their assets. We have been referred to your firm as a possible agent for this purpose."

"Can you share with me some of the particulars of what we are talking about? Is this trading company clients, for example? Or are there corporate entities involved?" Carmine said, waiting for the long translation.

"Mr. Chen has researched your firm and understands you specialize in complex leveraged buyouts for closely held companies. This is a similar kind of project, except it will require restructuring old corporations and holdings into new organizations and moving things across international borders."

Her companion interrupted her in Chinese for a moment and she then added, "Mr. Chen requires a very special legal agent for this project. He does not want publicity whatsoever about any of this. There can be no press or disclosure. If that were to happen he would terminate the relationship immediately and take action to remedy the damage. Are you clear on this, Mr. Salvatore?" Miss Carter said bluntly while she and Mr. Chen looked long and hard at Carmine.

Carmine fell into childhood memories of family discussions, thinking to himself how familiar it all sounded.

"I can assure you I can be very discrete as can all the members of this firm. We take client privilege very seriously and do not share any sensitive information with anyone outside that confidence."

Mr. Chen and the translator held a conversation in rapid Chinese before Mr. Chen spoke directly to Carmine this time.

"Mr. Salvatore, I speak direct now. Need someone who spend much time and work hard for us. I find out about you before I come. You know how keep secret and work very hard be good lawyer. Others here old and rich. Only want do things they know how. We want what they can do for us, but they hard understand what we want. Not understand tell no one our business."

Carmine thought for a moment about what to say next.

"Mr. Chen let me be direct also. I work for Mr. Hamilton directly and have his full confidence and can access any asset the firm has to offer for a client. I also treat every client and their business as proprietary and do not share any information I do not have to with others. But, again, Mr. Hamilton is my superior and will need to understand exactly what I am doing and for whom, so that it does not have an adverse impact on the firm, or that I might misrepresent the firm in a way that would lead to damage to it or its reputation. If you understand that then I would like to hear some actual details about your business, and what you think we can do to assist you legally."

Miss Carter spoke at length with Mr. Chen after translating and turned back to Carmine with a smile.

"We understand completely Mr. Salvatore. Anything less would be unacceptable to us. We require an honest broker that will represent our interests to your firm personally and forcefully. We would be paying for that and expect nothing less. You may be the right person and Mr. Chen is willing to give you that opportunity on a trial basis. Is that acceptable to you?"

"Yes. Now may we start?"

Mr. Chen opened his briefcase and handed Carmine a large file folder speaking to the translator for a moment.

"This is the first matter," Miss Carter said. "This is the file for Hodges Group Pty Ltd. It is an Australian holding company for various mining interests. The financial accounts are handled through Wells Fargo in Hong Kong. The corporation that holds Hodges is Li Hong Holdings Limited. Mr. Chen is the chairman. There are associated financial assets in Shanghai that are not deposited through Wells Fargo that are to be moved to San Francisco. The file contains information about those assets."

She added after a brief discussion with her companion: "We will need you to restructure the financial parts in Shanghai in particular into deposits and corporate entities in San Francisco that report to the Hong Kong holding corporation. We also wish for you to arrange an audit of the Australian holdings and advise Mr. Chen about any restructuring there that might be necessary."

This is a trial run? Carmine thought to himself. *I wonder what they consider full scale involvement? Hamilton is going to shit!*

"This is more – complicated. I will need a retainer to get started and will have many questions. Did you have a budget for this in mind?"

After a long discussion the translator said, "Mr. Chen is prepared to extend you a retainer of $100,000 USD to begin the work. The file contains contacts to start with for your initial work for the retainer. There are primary contacts for Li Hong, Hodges and Wells Fargo to get you started. Is this sufficient at this time?"

"Yes, yes it is, Mr. Chen, Miss Carter. You have left me with much to do. I will have my administrator arrange the retainer. How shall I contact you when it is ready?"

"We will be in New York for two more days. You may contact us at the New York Palace Hotel. There is mail, Telex and telephone information in the folder. Please provide a summary of the work to be performed per your understanding after reviewing the file, and the receipt for the retainer by 9 AM on Friday May 30ᵗʰ. You may courier the documents to me at the hotel. Miss Terry Carter, Room 518. Is there any other information you would like?"

"No, that should be enough to get me started. I will call you at the hotel if I have any questions."

"That will be acceptable. However, we may be out and you might not get an immediate response. We will expect the summary Friday morning in any case."

Carmine thought about what a summary meant in reality – detailed and accurate to the period he was sure. They were not kidding about this being a trial, and he was buried in Hamilton's work. He would be doing his own work on this one though. For $100,000 and a large new client of his own he was going to be here all night to get it done. This was his ticket to partner, or out on his own if he could pull it off.

***

"That was a large retainer, are you really sure about him?" Terry asked Fu-His in Chinese on the way to the elevator.

"Yes, I believe so. We have investigated him and believe he can be trusted. But we will have to test it."

"He never asked you if you were the head of all the companies you gave him to work on."

"That's part of the test. He cannot go very far with it. The CEO has been around for a very long time and this is only a tiny part."

"So I have heard. It all started with a Nevada gold mine I believe."

"He knows about it."

"Really? Isn't this just a small thing?"

"It's the small things that you have to pay the most attention to."

Terry smiled and they got on to the elevator.

***

"Carmine, I didn't know where you were," Carla said to him when he returned to his office after seeing his new client out. "Your aunt has been calling. She says it's urgent you call her right away. It sounds like it is."

"Hello, Aunt Adrianna, my secretary said you called," Carmine said in Italian into the phone after pushing aside the new stack of pink messages and moving three files off his chair so he could sit down.

"Carmine I have bad news. It's your mother. She had a heart attack and passed away this afternoon in the hospital. I'm so sorry. They called me when they could not reach you and want you to come right away."

Carmine sat stunned for a moment and finally said, "Thank you Adrianna. I'll get a flight. Which hospital is it?"

"Broward Health Medical Center, I did not write down the number right I was so upset. I'm so sorry. Let me find what I have."

"No, wait Adrianna, I can get the number. Don't worry now."

"Will you be able to get there today, Carmine? I hope so. Please call me when you know when the funeral is and anything I can do. This is very upsetting. I'm so sorry. My brothers were your father and step-father and Candy is family."

"I know, I know. I will get there Saturday," he said before thinking.

"Saturday! Oh, Carmine, this is your mother. Surely you can get there before then!"

"I'm sorry Adrianna, I shouldn't have said anything. It's business."

"Carmine. Your mother. Always business before family, just like your father, both of them. Always business. This is your mother, Carmine. Business can wait for once."

"Aunty Adrianna, I will call the hospital and the airline right now. I'll get there Saturday and take care of everything. Mother would understand."

"Oh, Carmine, Carmine. Goodbye," Adrianna said softly while hanging up.

Carmine had tears in his eyes while sorting messages and files to calm down before asking Carla to get the telephone number for the hospital and booking him a flight.

***

Selling Tony and Candy's house took Carmine longer than he expected. His father had passed in 1989 and Candy had kept the big house until now. By April the next year it finally sold and he could take the money along with what he had saved and get out of Hamilton and New York.

131

He talked Paul Arthur into coming with him. Fu-Hsi Chen approved of his quiet work for Li Hong Holdings and offered a silent investment to Carmine if he would structure his own firm in a way Fu could approve. Paul had done much of the business detailed planning for LHH and Fu approved of his choice as a partner. Carmine and Paul recruited another business planning specialist from a New York Real Estate firm that worked with HS&B on and off. John Reynolds specialized in international insurance and had a small Latin American client list he could bring to Salvatore, Arthur, and Reynolds.

Carmine and Paul tiptoed into South Florida in the spring of 1998, leaving New York and their past where it was. Their business with Fu and what he brought to the firm grew and grew with nary a ripple outside the walls of SA&R. John Reynolds was their face to the outside world. He circulated in society and when the firm did generate a business buzz it was how well they were growing in Latin America and how South Florida benefited as a gateway to the region.

***

"I have somebody you might want to meet," John said walking into Carmine's office.

"Hum, yes. What?" Carmine said looking up from behind his overflowing side table. The desk was worse. It served as a staging area where he threw things to sit before taking them to the large worktable along the wall where he liked doing most of his work. Only partners and his admin came into his office, except for Fu and Carmines personal clients who all closed the door and spent hours in there.

"You said last month at the partner meeting that you needed somebody to run around for you outside the firm. I may have a candidate for you."

"Uh, I was just venting about having to waste time going to meetings while work piled up. I don't know, you know what our clients expect. They would not be happy with just anybody showing up and saying, *trust me*. They pay us for that personal involvement."

"They pay *you*, Carmine. They want only you and you can't do the work and show up when they call for a meeting in God knows where at he same time."

"Exactly. They won't trust anybody else."

"Talk to her anyway. She's just like you. My niece went to law school with her in Arizona and told me she's the most secretive person she ever met. Sound familiar? Anyway, I checked up on her and talked to her on the phone. I think you should talk to her."

"Okay, I'll talk to her. But I don't think there really is anybody who can do the job."

"Her name is Marlana Garcia, here is her number in Arizona. I told her you would call Friday morning sometime."

"Oh, damn. What time did you tell her? I don't even have her resume. I need to think about this first."

"I gave Robyn everything and had her put it on your calendar. She'll forward it all along. Talk to her, you're too busy and we need more of your time here for the business. You are going to have to delegate something. Do it Carmine. I'm your partner and you need to."

"Yes, yes I'll talk to her," Carmine said looking back at his work. "I will."

***

"Hello Ms. Garcia, this is Carmine Salvatore of Salvatore, Arthur, and Reynolds," the formal voice spoke into Marlana's ear. "Are you by yourself?"

"What? Who? Hello, uh, Mr. Salvatore," Marlana said wondering who this was and almost hanging up the phone call with the *unknown* caller ID. "Yes, there is no one else with me." She remembered she had been expecting his call and his administrator had asked her to please be by herself when he called her.

"Very good. Thank you for arranging it. I want to protect your privacy, you understand. John Reynolds asked me to contact you, that you might be seeking employment after passing the bar."

Marlana's guard was up, her normal state since leaving college so long ago, back when she was another person.

"I am sorry Mr. Salvatore, I remember now that Mr. Reynolds said he would speak to his partner, but he did not give me a name.

"That is fair Ms. Garcia." Mr. Salvatore replied in a more direct tone. "I do not know you either other than a person my partner asked me to evaluate as a candidate we might want to hire. I, we, need a unique person for a discrete role we have been lacking for some time. Tell me what kind of position you are looking for and why we should hire you."

She was aware Mr. Salvatore was not anybody's jovial uncle. His words had a cool hardness to them as far as she was concerned. But she could sense a real question under it also. He was asking her something. She might be imagining that and reading too much into a distant voice over the telephone, but the feeling was there nonetheless.

"I just remembered something my mother said," Marlana said rising to the challenge.

"Yes?"

"He who speaks first loses."

"Ha," the voice answered with less coolness. "I'll take that. I have a very private client that requires much of my time. I need to find an assistant who can work with them in a direct fashion and report accurately what they need to me, as well as assisting me in executing whatever it turns out to be. The right person is very – very flexible and can read some very confusing tea leaves quickly and give the correct information to the client on the spot. They will have to find information when there isn't any and get secretive people to tell them things. It's not a conventional job for an average attorney, let alone one just out of law school. Why would I consider you for it?"

"Because is sounds like you need a good spy who only trusts as far as she can reach out her arm. You also want somebody who understands just how twisted things get if she forgets to pay attention, think things out to their logical conclusion, and doesn't do what's necessary to get them there. You want somebody who has real experience at doing difficult things alone. I've been there."

"Why did you become a lawyer?"

"To understand how to avoid trouble and deal with it when it comes. Because I believe people will cheat you or worse when they can. You need to learn how to deal with them in an organized way using the weight of society rather than just your own personal strength. That's how you win."

"That sounds more personal, Ms. Garcia. What about helping clients?"

Marlana flinched mentally at having let her feelings respond instead of giving a more arms length answer.

"The client is the one with the problem, always. You have to advocate for them and use your experience and training to help them solve their issues. They come to you because they have a problem and you are the one who has to find the answer. That is always paramount."

"I liked your first answer better. It was a personal question and you answered it directly. I can meet with the first person if she would come to our offices day after tomorrow at two PM."

"I will be there."

"Very good. I *will* look forward to meeting you," Carmine said and hung up.

Bastard! Marlana thought putting down the phone. She smiled and muttered with a laugh, "Test me you will, you're going to pay for this. Fuck, more on the credit card. And, I have to get to Florida – *and* he didn't give me an address. What a prick, and he wants me to work for him!"

Mike Macartney

Chapter 14
Lanarkshire Scotland 1887

Robert McKean left Lanarkshire, Scotland, to find gold in America in the spring of 1887 when he was 17 years old. He had been working in the coal pits since he was 13, like his father before him and his grandfather too. Even though both parent and grandparent had been born after the colliers were freed from indentured servitude to the pits, they stayed and worked them along with all the aunts and uncles, brothers and sisters, and cousins.

His father always talked of going to America, so when he died of consumption Robert said goodbye to his remaining two brothers and three sisters and went south to Kirkcudbright with his life savings to find gold in America. He borrowed everything he could from his kin on the promise to pay back in full when he struck it rich in the new world and could help them come too. He left County Lanark with almost £5, more money than he had ever seen before.

The steerage fare to America cost him £3.10s and he was expected to supply all his own mess utensils, bedding, and any other items he would need for the 12-day voyage. He got water and a ration of food from the ship. Nothing would be sold on the ship and he had to live on what he brought and the rations he was given. To book passage he had to prove himself not infirmed, deaf, blind, or over 60 years of age so as not to become a public charge in America.

"There could be a short wait before sailing," the ticket master said to Robert after he had taken his money and issued the ticket for America.

"I do not understand, sir?"

137

"The crew, well the Captain may have to assure the crew is ready and everything is prepared on the ship."

"Aye. I hope the wait inna long. Be there something wrong with the ship?" Robert said worrying about his depleted funds and what he would do if it turned out to be a long time before sailing. He figured he could sleep by the docks and save everything for when he arrived in America.

A small whirlwind in a blue uniform screeched through the door to the ticket masters tiny office accompanied by scorching blasts of profanity that Robert had not heard since he left the colliery.

"Why those bleeding low life arses that canna stay away from their bleeding liquor the day before sailing. Worthless scum that shulda be keelhauled iffin' I hada been on the sea, by God. Damn their eyes."

"Captain Clarke, this passenger was just asking about the timetable," the ticket master said to the red faced being.

"I dunna care. I havta find stokers now. Two a' the useless bleeders beat each others bein' drunk n' canna work at all. I put out'a call on the dock, but they'll be worthless layabouts that is left now."

"Captain, I'll work. I be used to it," Robert said to the Captain thinking that he needed to sail now and every penny he earned would matter when he got off the ship.

The Captain squinted at Robert with a hard stare before asking, "You e'er been t'sea, Boy? You look a landlubber. The sea's hard Boy n' I got no use for sumin' that dunna can stand it, n' be lazy n' pukin' o'er the side. They'll be lazy I can find here. Well, boy, speak up."

"Uh, Captain, I been workin' the pits since I was thirteen. Nobody e'er call me lazy or scared. I can work n' I need work."

The Captain glared at Robert some more before saying he should go onboard and find the chief engineer Alexander Outterridge. If he could use Robert then he would agree, but it would be fourteen hours every day, and if he got the seasickness he would be expected to work no matter.

Robert did manage to convince the ship's engineer into letting him feed the ship's boilers every day to save 10 shillings off the fare, and he would work no matter what. The engine room engineer liked him and taught him the job of not just shoveling coal but pitching and patching the fire bed evenly, raking out clinkers, and banking the fire correctly front to back.

The *Elegant Lady* sailed on schedule, one stoker short.

Robert hated coal, but shoveling it into the ships boilers was much easier than working the pits. The seasickness made the first few days bad and he had to learn to stagger and roll with the ship so as to not fall into hot steam pipes or the side of the boilers. The trip went smoothly for the rest of the passengers and no fog greeted them in the harbor of New York.

He funneled off the ship and onto ferries to Castle Gardens, where he proved his health to a busy doctor, slept on the floor for a day while he exchanged his English money for American money, and headed off to find the Brooklyn, Bath and Coney Island Railroad.

Alexander was an American. He father had come to New York City from Scotland as an indentured servant thirty-three years earlier. When the Captain could not convince Robert to sign on for the return trip to England, he gave Robert a letter to take to his brother-in-law. It said Robert was a hard worker, had worked for him as a fireman on his ship, and was a quick learner. He sent Robert to a new hotel at a place called Coney Island.

Alexander's sister had married the older man who built the Hayling Hotel, and he knew they had a steam train from New York City to bring people to the hotel. He explained to Robert that nobody got a job without knowing somebody to help him. He liked Robert and he worked harder than his usual crew. Alexander told Robert to talk to his brother-in-law about a job shoveling coal on an American railroad when he got port and give him the letter of introduction. That was Robert's first lesson about America and New York City. Robert promised to bring Alexander the best bottle of whiskey he could find – he understood the lesson.

Robert stepped off the ferry in the new world on May 3, 1887 with $2 and 14¢ in his pocket and a person to contact for a job shoveling coal.

***

Robert shoveled coal on the train, back and forth between the city and the beach, from 6 AM until 6 PM six days a week for $1.34 a day. He found a room in an attic of a Lower East Side house with four families in it. He paid $1.75 a month for the room.

He knew he would never go far in the new world unless he could understand it, and to do that he would need to learn to read. He heard about a new thing called a "Settlement House" that had opened the year before near his room, He went there to learn about America and how to read whenever he could.

Robert's father had always taught him to never trust anybody outside the blood family, and not trust them much either. The money he saved to go to California, where the gold was, he hid under a loose floorboard in his room. He worried about it every day going to work in case somebody found it or the rooming house burned. He thought about burying it in the tiny weed patch behind the house, but there were too many eyes watching. He told people in the house he was out looking for work every day and never bought new things so they would not think he had any money. He didn't pay his rent on time, waiting until the landlord yelled about it.

A conductor he talked to on the train explained that in America banks were not safe, you always had to pay attention. They had failed in 1873 and never fully recovered. He could leave his money in them as long as he watched what was happening and was ready to run down and get it out if it looked like they were in trouble. After much worrying, Robert finally put his money in a bank. The fear about hiding it in his room and being found out had become too much to bear, even if the banks were always shaky. He made sure to talk to the managers at his bank and to even eventually the president. He would hear about trouble sooner that way.

Robert had less work in the winter when the trains ran less often. By March 1888, he had spent some of his savings and started working part-time for the engineer on his train to learn the job. The conductor who ran the train disliked the engineer who drank too much and ignored him. He thought it was his train, not the conductor's. William "Billy" Burnie, the conductor, came from Glasgow and Thomas Youngston, the engineer, came from Cornwall. He had never met a Scotsman he could trust, especially Billy. Billy liked Robert though, and he put him in the middle of their feud with the intent of getting rid of Thomas when the opportunity presented itself.

Thomas treated Robert like the ignorant coal miner he thought of him as. He threatened him with falling under the train if he did not keep quiet about the drinking or do what he was told, his thick Scottish head would never understand any of it anyway.

Robert picked up the engineer's job very quickly and kept his head down around Thomas, pretending difficulty with learning how to drive a train. He only talked to Billy when the engineer would not see them together and told Thomas how much he, too, hated the conductor when he could.

Billy had arranged for the railroad to pay Robert his fireman's wages while learning the job so long as he never told Thomas. He was to say he would come in and help him for free if he could learn from him about being an engineer. Robert would pay Billy 20¢ a day when he worked for the engineer.

"Nobody'll 'ere give ye nuthin' less ye make'em," Robert's father always told him. "They'll make'ya work free if the' kin. Dunna err letum do that to ye, son."

Robert always asked to be paid no matter what others did or were afraid to do. His father's words never failed him, and when he got scared he remembered working deep underground when it was 100 degrees and the timbers cracked and snapped letting dirt and rocks fall on him, snuffing out his lamp and everybody else yelling and running the other way to leave him there.

He also worked odd jobs in addition to the railroad when he could at the Hayling Hotel whose owner had recommended him to the railroad in the first place. He made a point of talking to everyone and always kept track of his debts to people who had helped him. He stayed in touch with all of them when he could, all the way back to the times when he worked the pits. He could work at the hotel and sleep in the room for the staff when he worked there.

James Conover built the hotel with money he made selling soap. His father had come with James his mother, and his three younger sisters from Ireland during the starving time when the potato crop failed and worked as a gandy dancer on the railroad. The Conovers lived in the Fourth Ward where the Whyo gang first recruited James because of his hulking size, later for his brains. For all his physical menace James preferred less overt methods. He decided to tie local soap makers and slingers together with the help of his gang connections. Making soap was a dirty and difficult thing people were happy to turn over to others in the expanding new nation. The soap makers went along most of the time, and James quickly learned to always pay Tammany Hall their cut of the business along with the Whyos. James never got too greedy either, so his business did not have problems, like fires and frightened customers others had.

Maybe James recognized a kindred spirit in Robert or just maybe he liked having the kid listen to him over a drink or three or four at the hotel. "Always remember your friends, and share your good fortune with them," he would say. "Never trust a politician unless you pay them, and then trust them even less. It is not what you know; it is who you know boy. And I think you already understand that. Just remember it though. It does not matter if they call you an Irish dog or 'that Mick son-of-a-bitch' just smile and take their money boy."

Sharon Lang lived in Room 218 in the back corner of the second floor at the Hayling. There were three other *Sharons* on that floor that James brought from San Francisco to entertain guests in his hotel. James never had an issue with the police. The local commissioner, John McLane, ate with James at the hotel dining room every month and enjoyed the second floor delights himself on his visits.

Sharon also worked for the other women on the second floor and took care of keeping their clothes and rooms up to the standards James set for his business. She collected the money from the customers for James.

"Do you fancy her boy?" James asked Robert when Sharon passed through the back of the lobby where they sat.

"Uh, well, she is pretty," Robert stuttered with a rare failure of words.

"Ha, that she is boy. Don't be fooled though. She's harder than a flint. It's five dollars to visit her, if you like." James never passed by a buck no matter who he made it from.

"Five dollars! That's a lot of money Mr. Conover. More than I make in a whole week most of the time."

"Well boy, she's special, and I had to bring her all the way from San Francisco. The snow is starting to pile up and the wind is about to rip the roof off. You better plan on being here for a spell. I'll need you to shovel and look after things. And boy?"

"Yes, Mr. Conover?"

"She's in Room 218," James said laughing at Robert's red face and discomfiture.

Robert awoke early the next morning to help the hotel staff deal with the snow and the few guests who could not leave the hotel. Robert spent the next three days lighting fires, cleaning fireplaces, moving wood, heating water, fixing shutters and windows, cleaning snow off roofs, and lighting kerosene lamps when the gas to the hotel stopped.

Two weeks later to the day Robert made it back to his cold room in the Lower East Side. After five days at the hotel he sloughed through a maze of snow walled streets with fallen power, telephone, and telegraph lines, especially in the downtown. He spent the next nine days digging out the trains and the tracks all the way into New York. The snow defeated even the biggest locomotives and the workers heard one in New York had derailed when it tried to push through the snow. The train companies did not pay him, only a room and food on pain that if the trains did not run he did not have a job.

By April the trains ran again and most electric, telephone, and telegraph lines had been re-suspended, lights came back and only the hard, dirty ice passages remained. The newspapers continued to scream about the electricity wires and putting them and the transportation system out of harm's way, underground, despite the injunctions against the laws enacted to force electric companies to install underground wiring. After the "Great White Hurricane" of 1888 snow would haunt the mayors of New York City from then on.

Robert became the youngest engineer on the railroad in the fall, for a wage of $2.65 per day. He agreed to pay Billy $.25 a day for one month for helping him get the job. He spent 9s. 4d. for a weighted onyx walking stick with a silver head he ordered from T. Briggs & Son in London for James. He bought good whiskey that cost $1.49 a bottle to take to the engineer and the Captain on the *Elegant Lady* who docked in New York in December.

He had established a line of credit at his bank for his family in County Lanark to pay back the money he had borrowed from them. He had found no gold in America other than work shoveling coal and living in a cold room in a crowded city. Most of his kith had families now to support. The work in the collieries had improved slowly with increases in coal prices, larger trade unions, and power in the parliament. Talking about getting rich in America and actually leaving home to get rich there turned out to be two different things. Only a cousin two years older than Robert wanted to come over. The whiskey might help smooth his trip.

***

The birth of a new century came and went while Robert first drove railroad engines, then conducted trains, and finally bought them with his own money and the money he borrowed. He never forgot surviving the fear of being buried in the absolute blackness of a coal mine whenever he ran with money from the bankers he had befriended, who taught him their business, or from the people like James and the local machine commissioners and politicians that came with them, who taught him *their* kind of business. He bought parts of this train company, or that ferry line in bankruptcy, or the cargos his friends in the shipping business brought from wherever they found them with the money he supplied. He won his bets more than lost, but he always paid the people who mattered their cut first. When he could not and everybody lost something they trusted him because of it – and kept telling him things and letting him on their schemes and secrets that he always paid them back for. His father's advice never failed him.

Robert helped a few others of his family back at the pits when they showed promise like his cousin who now was the chief engineer on a luxury liner out of Liverpool. He gave a pittance to others too, just in case they might have some information he could use. They never did and were happy enough to live out their lives digging coal and drinking at the pubs for as long as their backs, lungs, and livers lasted. Bankers in Scotland chased him to invest in the pits themselves with his gold from America, but he hated coal far too much for that. Gold never could get the black dust off his hands.

By 1905 Robert McKean Equities kept his office at the Equitable Life Assurance Building at the bottom of Manhattan Island. There were newer and grander buildings going up all around, and Robert even invested in some of them. He would hate having to move and to spend more money on a new office when his free one was just fine.

He provided *investment advice* for the life insurance company and the flamboyant James Hazen Hyde, the Equitable CEO. The relationship brought his current issue with the State of New York.

"Mr. McKean, I believe you did attend the party in January, and you do have an office here which you pay less than the market rent for," John Thomas said across the desk in Robert's office. "The State of New York is very concerned about any hint of malfeasance in something as important as the insurance industry is to the State. I am sure you understand that. Now what else can you tell me about Mr. Hyde and this affair?"

"John, I'm sorry, I was only a guest at Mr. Hyde's ball. I received an invitation like anybody else. I rented costumes for myself and my wife Sharon so we could attend.
It was a very nice affair, but I was only a guest and have no knowledge of any of the particulars of it."

"It certainly *should* have been. It cost $200,000 of the company's money. For a *costume* party."

"Oh no, I can't believe it cost anything like that amount. I certainly have no idea how it was paid for. I do not work for Equitable and I just assumed Mr. Hyde paid for it all himself for. If he didn't, then it's news to me."

"Hum, now if that's all you are going to say at this point. Why *do you* have an office here at all Mr. McKean? Like you say, you aren't an employee of Equitable Life Assurance. I am having great difficulty understanding why you are here at all then."

"Mr. Thomas, as you know I advise Equitable about the railroad industry in particular, and they appreciate my advice. I do pay for my office space and I have other work I do here, besides Equitable. They are my client and good enough to rent me office space."

"Rent? We have found no evidence that you pay any rent. Do you have receipts you wish to show me?

"I would have to find them."

"I will want them, Mr. McKean. Now tell me about your relationship with Mr. Hyde. You advise him about railroads and where he should spend Equitable's money then, do you?"

"Oh certainly not. I advise Equitable and Mr. Hyde is party to it. I am sure the Board of Directors of Equitable considers advice from many other people, as well as their own employees, and Mr. Hyde too. They make decisions on much more than just my simple ideas. I am only an advisor."

"Mr. McKean you also are party to some of these investments you advise about, aren't you? And, you have other people putting money into them besides Equitable Life Assurance and Mr. Hyde. Isn't that true?"

"You have to be specific about what you are talking about, Mr. Thomas. If you could show me something to help me understand better maybe I could help you. I'm at a loss right now about exactly what you are asking?"

"I see. We *will* find out and I *will* be back to talk to you then, Mr. McKean. The Board of Directors and the State of New York are very upset about just how Mr. Hyde has handled company funds, and you seem to be part of all of it. I will be back again, you can be certain it."

"Then I will expect you to have some documents to show me at that point, Mr. Thomas, so that I might assist you and the State of New York to get to the bottom of whatever concerns you. But I am positive it is nothing I would have any direct knowledge of or would be of very much help on. I'm sorry. I'm at a loss about how to assist you without more information myself."

"Good day, Mr. McKean."

"Good day, Mr. Thomas."

Shortly thereafter James Hazen Hyde left the presidency of The Equitable and forty-odd other companies he sat on the Board of and moved to France. Robert closed his office at the Equitable Building taking a space in the back of the World Building on Park Row. He did not move in right away, deciding he and his wife had earned a vacation. They packed up and took a leisurely six-day Pullman train trip to Chicago and then on to San Francisco. He had always wanted to find gold in America. This was his first chance to actually go to the place where so much of it ended up from the mines of California and Nevada. He had learned during his time in America that the real wealth existed in where the gold went and who used it in places like San Francisco, rather than finding it on the ground or digging it out of a hot, wet Stygian hole in the ground. It was just like coal in that way. He understood coal.

Robert visited his one of his business friends at United Railroads in San Francisco for a wonderful dinner and a business meeting to discuss possible new investment by some of his clients in New York. He discovered good opportunities for projects in the central valleys of California near the state capital of Sacramento, as well as the building of underground trollies in San Francisco once the mayor and supervisors approved them. The railroad worked directly with the Mayor's personal attorney, Mr. Ruef, and had made civic improvements in lighting and incurred other expenses to secure the approval.

He had created small accounts at San Francisco National Bank for his business in California. He added to them just in case while on his vacation from New York. Bankers everywhere always had good ideas for him and his money. He made a small investment of his own money in one the San Francisco bankers recommended.

The investment made Mr. McKean a paid consultant and President of a small mining company in Sacramento, California: McKean Mining and Tool. The company had a gold mining operation in the neighboring state of Nevada at the recent strike in Goldfield. With a population of almost 20,000 and three new rail lines there, the potential existed for this to rival the Comstock of half a century before. Robert understood railroads too.

Robert's investment would be paid back in three years and his salary would continue for five years thereafter to be renegotiated if the firm remained profitable.

Two white banks held an interest in the company, and some Chinaman from the Canton Bank of San Francisco, which had the largest share, explained the deal to Robert. He never had much to do with the Chinese in New York. There were a lot more of them in San Francisco, but they guaranteed his salary while his bank held an escrow account with enough in it to cover a year's wages. San Francisco National had money in the Chinese firm and stood by the accounting. They said they would all make money.

"So this Dan Chen is the owner of the Tonopah, Nevada mine you want me to be the president of?" Robert asked the Chinese banker.

"Dong Chen, yes he invests in the mining in Nevada. As I said he has put the money for your salary in your bank, I believe," the banker said looking at the nodding San Francisco National men.

"Dong, Dan. Okay. I would like to meet him," Robert said with narrowed eyes.

"I am sorry Mr. McKean, but Mr. Chen is traveling to Chicago and cannot be here for a few weeks. He has given me his full confidence and would hope that you would be willing to start now and will be able to meet with him when he returns to San Francisco."

"And when will that be? I like to look people I do business with in the eye, you understand."

"Of course you do Robert," a San Francisco National banker broke in. "I have met Mr. Chen on this and he has business with our bank too. I can vouch for him and that this is a solid arrangement for everyone. We would not be investing in it if it was not."

Hum, well George I hope so. I have a great deal of money at your bank and want to do other investing with you. I don't like to lose money," Robert said looking hard at the banker who nodded with a wan smile. The Chinese banker sat expressionless as Robert watched him out of the corner of his eyes to gauge his response.

"Okay, Wu," Robert said turning to the quiet San Francisco banker. "You have a deal. But I want to meet Chen as soon as he gets back to San Francisco.

"I understand completely, Mr. McKean. I will arrange it immediately. I am very happy you are doing this."

The three smiling bankers all shook hands with the coal miner. He finally had his gold mine in America.

Robert McKean died on April 18, 1906 at the age of 46 when his roof fell in on him at his home on Nob Hill during the earthquake. His wife Sharon survived and lived well in her native New York until 1934. She died a wealthy woman at 78 years of age. Robert had bought a large life insurance policy in New York to provide for her. The banks in San Francisco fought her inheritance claims, but a mining company in Nevada provided her with a salary for a few years they said her husband had earned. She did not ask about it. There were many things about Robert she had learned not to ask about.

Chapter 15
Las Vegas, Nevada Tuesday July 22, 2014

Calliope sat down in the front seat of the dusty silver Toyota Corolla with the big female driver. She was sure the young woman with the brown ponytail had been the same one who took her back to the hotel after the excitement of the previous evening.

"Your luggage from the hotel is in the back," the woman said to her when she buckled into the driver's side. The disassembled bicycle and the luggage panniers sat on the seat behind them.

Cally felt better seeing her things and escaping from the stress of the hotel meeting. She began to think again and puzzle out what might be happening in this strange case with so many blind alleys. Usually the initial confusion of a new assignment cleared in a logical way, and she could see an end somewhere down the road. The walls of this maze towered over her, behind her, and in front of her. Twists and turns did not form a path but appeared all of a sudden out of a gray haze. The nebulous way forward meant stepping in one direction while looking down at her feet to not step into nothing.

"Where are we headed, Miss?"

The woman smiled, sort of, over towards her with a laugh, sort of. "We are taking a trip, or at least you are."

Calliope gulped and turned and looked behind her seat. "Is there somebody with a wire behind me?"

"Ha, maybe you will enjoy the trip after all. This is not one of those mafia rides. I am just the driver. You can relax."

"You also drove me to the hotel last night, didn't you?'

"It looks like you have enough in your bags for a few days. You can buy what else you might need there. I have your passport." The woman said reaching into the door tray and passing Calliope's passport over to her. She started the car and drove out of the parking lot.

"My house is alarmed and I have a private security service to look after things."

"Yes, so I was told."

The driver stayed on Las Vegas Boulevard heading south and said nothing more. She turned east and drove into a large business jet hanger at the Henderson Executive Airport.

The driver parked behind a pristine white G650 Gulfstream business jet and told Calliope to grab her bags and follow her onto the aircraft.

"Please have a seat Ms. Dancer," Marlana said to her when Cally stepped into the front of the plane. "We are waiting for the crew. You can stow your bags in the closet at the rear. It will be the three of us and the pilots for the flight." She looked at Calliope's driver.

"I apologize for the short notice Allison. Do you have your overnight gear?"

"Yes, Ma'am, oh Marlana. Sorry, old habits."

"Ha, You can take the girl out of the Army, but you can't take the Army out of the girl."

Calliope walked past Marlana who sat on a leather couch seat along the side of the elegant passenger compartment where she could see the length of the interior and the entrance door.

Cally returned and sat facing forward at one end of where Marlana sat and Allison sat facing aft towards them at the other. A low, narrow teak table framed the group.

It will be a long flight Ms. Dancer. About 14 hours give or take. You have the run of the cabin and a berth can be opened if you wish," Marlana said to her with a lighter, more open mood than the cold evaluation at the hotel.

"Where are we going?"

"Shanghai, China. Have you been?"

"No, Hong Kong and Beijing, but not Shanghai. So that is why you *found* my passport for me."

"Yes. You have a very nice home and security system. Don't be concerned. Nothing else was disturbed, we only needed your passport."

"You have an efficient organization. Ex-military bodyguards," Calliope said nodding at Allison. "People to call who can penetrate a secured residence in another city and have things delivered from it – and this plane," she added looking up and around before focusing back on Marlana.

"You manage the same yourself for just one person. You have an interesting *practice*, if you call it that."

"Yes, my life takes me a lot of places and I meet a lot of different people all over. You have been one of the more confusing ones," Calliope said relaxing for the first time in all her encounters with Marlana.

"I could say the same about you. Some of your clients, the recent ones in particular, are very unusual. The woman last night for example, and that charmer in Reno. You seem to attract them."

Cally tried not to show any response to how much this woman knew, and why she had never heard of her before. There were not many who were aware of people like Samantha and Tyrone, let alone knew the particulars of their lives.

"People hire me because I can manage their affairs with people like Tyrone and Samantha. It's a talent."

"Those psychoactive sweets you hand out to everybody help quite a bit too, I expect."

Cally twitched. "Um, I do like to make candy and people seem to enjoy it. I don't know how psychoactive it is, but you know how addictive chocolate is," she said with a big smile and a toss of her head.

"I had an analysis done. They are quite a concoction, those *chocolate* candies, very sophisticated to say the least, he told me. They may have saved you."

"Saved me? How do you mean that?" Cally said with a mixture of suspicion and fear.

"Since we have come this far ... your network and customers are not the kind we normally want to deal with. We would typically *neutralize* them, but that bit of chemistry you gave me a few weeks ago proved very interesting. Very. If you have the abilities you appear to, as well as the tools to do what you do, along with your penetration of certain groups that might be a bother to us, then we might have something to talk about with you."

"Okay, well, would you elaborate just what you are saying?"

"I have a job to do Ms. Dancer."

"Calliope."

"Calliope. You're sophisticated. You can separate or balance the needs of your customers from your own management of them. You don't let your preconceived notions drive you. That's a valuable skill. We can use it – even if it sounds like some silly spy movie, if you get my drift," Marlana said, laughing finally. "There's a long story there, believe me. If I were to tell — oh good the crew is here."

Two uniformed Chinese men had stepped through the door with flight bags and luggage interrupting the conversation. Marlana stood up to greet them while Cally tried not to show her frustration at having to drop the discussion right when she seemed to be getting somewhere.

"Don't worry, there is a long trip ahead," Allison said watching Calliope and her expression. She knew her job.

No wonder Marlana's relaxed for a change. Hum, she speaks Chinese. This gets weirder and weirder.

The pilots looked Calliope over while talking to Marlana and went to the flight deck. A soft jerk a few minutes later and the aircraft rolled out of the hanger and stopped for engine start and final checks on the ramp before taxing to the end of the long runway.

"Buckle up," Marlana said.

"I am," Cally said and Allison just replied, "Set."

The sleek jet rolled around the end of the taxiway, lined up with the runway and accelerated down it in one smooth action. The plane lifted up sharply and banked north to begin the long flight to China.

"I am going to sack out for a few, Ally. It was a long night. You got it?" Marlana said to her.

"Yes, Ma'am … Marlana."

"I'll spell you then. I don't think there is too much to worry about though."

"I'm used to it. I thought I was back in Iraq last night for a minute. We could have used you there," Allison said turning to Calliope.

"Ha! You didn't have enough lawyers there?"

"Not if we could help it," Allison said laughing. "They can't shoot straight."

"Stop right there! We're not that crooked!"

Marlana got up still chuckling and headed aft to open a berth.

"You can sack out too, if you want to," Allison said to Calliope.

"No, I'm okay. I got some sleep at the hotel."

"That's more than we had. I wasn't expecting ten rounds downrange out the car door. It wasn't about you, you were okay."

"I don't remember being told that."

"I suppose so. It wouldn't have any difference."

"What, difference, what?"

"Your gun."

Calliope hid her surprise, remembering the car being ripped apart and then the Chief and Samantha likewise. *Maybe it wouldn't have.*

"What did happen there? It wasn't just a

traffic accident was it?"

"No, it wasn't"

It's like pulling teeth. Not as bad as Marlana at least. "Was it some kind of military system, like one of those mechanical power suits that people wear to give them super powers?"

"I'm just the security detail. I can't say. Ms. Garcia will have to brief you." Allison said with half of a smile.

Shit, she's no better after all.

Calliope switched tack and asked Allison more about herself; maybe she would be a little more open about that.

It took some time, but she finally pieced together that Allison Cohen had joined the Army right after September 11ᵗʰ, having watched the towers collapse on television from San Diego. Her father had retired there from the Navy. He spent the morning with her calling old military friends about which bases had put up fighter caps, and what was truly going on everywhere on that eventful day. Allison enlisted in the Army on September 12ᵗʰ.

Allison deferred her enlistment to finish her Civil Engineering degree at UC San Diego and two years later the Army sent her to basic training and Officers School then to Kuwait as a second lieutenant. Her engineering group supported the long logistics tail of the forces preparing to invade Iraq two years later. In ten months she found herself in Kirkuk in Northern Iraq protecting oil fields, then in Mosul by late 2004 commanding fuel trucks.

1ˢᵗ Lieutenant Allison suffered multiple fractures, internal injuries, and a detached retina at the end of 2005, when the truck in front of her hit an IED and her Humvee rolled off into the scrub beside the road.

When she returned to active duty the Army shipped her to Fort Benning to train new logistics specialists for the Iraq and Afghanistan operations. She went to Afghanistan in late 2007 to plan for the delivery of the new Mine-Resistant Ambush Protected vehicles arriving there. Her active duty enlistment was up in 2008, but she got *stop lost* for two more years of the Afghanistan War anyway.

Captain Cohen left the Army in 2010 to find a civilian job after almost decade in the Army and a lifetime out of school, a degree she had never used, and a purple heart and two campaign medals that nobody looking to hire her cared about.

"I met Marlana at a training program for executive protection a friend from the Army taught. He got me a gig there while I was looking for work on the outside."

"So you work for her, as a bodyguard?"

"Sort of. My job is more than that. Not just for her. I see she's up and I want some rack time," Allison said standing up when Marlana returned to their seats up front.

Hum, not just her. She didn't mean to say that. I should open the door and walk out of here, but this is finally getting interesting – maybe.

Calliope ratted through her bag and came up with a cherry surprise to cheer her up and get her feet planted back on the ground for the trip.

"Yum, I needed that," she said to Marlana when she sat down. "Would you like one? These are some of my specials."

"Yes, I'm sure they are. So, you have more of them, different ones?"

"Oh yes, of course, many. My great aunt had a talent and I cooked up some of my own too," she said with a wistful smile.

"I am sure you did. To each his own."

One of the pilots came back through the forward galley behind the flight deck and spoke to Marlana in Chinese with a big smile on his rugged face.

Oh my, he's flirting with her. How very interesting.

Cally wiggled down into her warm, soft

leather seat and started to enjoy herself again. Her usual confidence seeped back and she saw levels and shades again, not the confused tunnel vision accompanying her immediate personal survival that had dominated her meetings with this woman recently. *Ah, this is better. At last! She's actually going to tell me something, or take me to it.*

"You look more relaxed for a change," Marlana said flicking her eyes over her. "I'm glad you chose to. You've been a lot of work."

"I do – it's my job. Like yours taking care of extraordinary things, only different clients," Cally said smiling. "I am a little less hard edged about mine though."

"Oh please, clients? A Sig in your purse sitting next to those two sweethearts on the backside of Las Vegas? Ha-ha!" Marlana said laughing again.

"They pay the bills. Why are we going to China? It's not exactly what I expected, but not much surprises me at this point either."

"China, it's part of a long story. You'll find out soon enough. You have an interesting resume from what we have determined. Your network is quite extensive for someone so young, and you keep secrets well, considering. You understand what those secrets are worth too. Those are not talents everybody has, and that's attractive to us – provided you are very honest in whatever dealings we have. It may be a test you fail, but worth a chance. This isn't like your usual work, let's say."

"Usual? For me normal isn't. Never has been. You know you're still not telling me much. We were talking about why China, Shanghai I gather – and you speaking Chinese too. What's it about?"

"That's where is becomes an ancient story, and not one I know everything about to be honest. I work for a large business enterprise in Shanghai and they have decided you should come to the mountain to make up their minds about you in person."

I don't know if she is honest or does not really

know. Damn. Maybe she is just hired help too. "So I will be meeting with people who run this business, and they had you bring me?"

"What were you doing in China the last time, visiting one of your *clients*?"

"Sort of, I met some people who asked if I could help them with some political issues. I never did get back, it's a little out of my line, not strictly business."

"I would guess your candy would be exactly what politicians would want themselves."

"It really doesn't work that way. It's a personal thing, not just chemical. It's hard to explain it."

"I suppose, if you say so. I deal in more concrete things in my work."

"What is your work exactly? You are an attorney and travel a lot, but that's about all I know."

"I handle the day-to-day details for business transactions," Marlana said after hesitating for a moment. "Since you will know anyway, my work it is more than just the contracts and agreements. I am a trusted agent when the parties can't always show up themselves to make a deal."

"Yes, I get it. We may not be all that different in that. I help some of my customers understand the forces if you will, the environment around them and their business they don't always appreciate. Ecosystem advisor maybe is more like it."

Allison returned and joined into what then became a light discussion. Calliope tipped her chair back to doze while everyone waited out the long flight.

***

"Where are we landing?" Calliope asked when the Gulfstream dropped down into the landing pattern over a gray ocean of buildings, roads, and humanity punctuated with jutting spires of the new China. Towers stood smiling with jack-o'-lantern teeth of light and dark squares in a luminous cloud of smog as the night greeted the sun.

"Hongquiao International," Marlana said. "We'll take a short helicopter ride to Pudong."

"Not Shanghai?"

"Yes it is, the new business district with all those towers by the river you see there," Marlana said pointing out of the window at the river reflecting the early light.

"Then what?"

"Shower, food, and a bed. You will meet people tomorrow evening."

In the hanger the pilot again made a point of coming back to chat up Marlana. Calliope thought she enjoyed it this time. *She's finally letting her guard down a little. Yay! Now we can maybe get somewhere.*

When they stepped out of the White Airbus EC145 helicopter onto the helipad atop of one skyscraper among many, a blond woman in a black knit business suit came forward offering her hand to Calliope. "Hello, Miss Dancer. Welcome to Shanghai," she said. I am Terry Carter, I will be assisting you with your stay along with any Chinese language translations you might need."

"Oh, thank you. I do not speak Chinese. But, I assumed Ms. Garcia and Ms. Cohen would be showing me around?"

"They will be available, but right now I'm your tour guide and translator," Terry said with a big smile and cool green eyes.

Minder that is. "That will be nice. Are you taking me to my room then?"

"Yes I am. I expect that you would like to freshen up after the long trip."

"I would love to. Show me the way," Calliope said with her own toothy grin.

Terry led her to the roof elevator and they dropped down two floors by themselves in the elevator car. When the doors opened they stepped out onto black stone framed by dark wood panels and delicate white light from lamps in brass fixtures on the wall. A spray of white flowers on a black lacquered table under an ink painting of two cranes greeted them. The small lobby gave way to thick red and black carpeted hallways in two directions.

"Here is your room," Terry said unlocking a dark wooden door with recessed panels and a small placard indicating *Guest 3* in Chinese and English.

"Thank you Terry. Is there a plan, a schedule for me?"

"You will have the day tomorrow for yourself to adjust to Chinese time and crossing the date line. There is a telephone in the room and a menu if you want something to eat, like room service in a hotel. You can reach me on my cell. I have left my number next to the phone for you.

"There is a pool, sauna, steam room, and a gym. Feel free to use any of them."

"I may want to go out and walk around a little, if that's okay."

"Oh, certainly. There will be a dinner at 1800, 6:00PM for you, tomorrow evening where you will meet some of the other guests. It will be business formal. If you do not have the wardrobe then please give the concierge a call and they will be able to get you anything you need."

"I do have one good outfit that may work. I don't think I will need anything."

"I believe we have you at a size 10 with a 29-inch inseam, size 8 shoes. The concierge can provide anything you need."

"I'll think about it. My wardrobe was pretty casual for Las Vegas and had to all fit in my bike bags," Calliope said with a smile. *And no, I did not miss that you have my exact size, just in case I might want wander off alone from my room.* "Oh, and did my bicycle come on the plane?"

"No, I am sorry I had intended to tell you, the ground crew missed putting it on. They usually don't do things like that. I'm sorry. Nonetheless, the concierge can find you one in a day or two if you need it, although I would not recommend riding around Shanghai unless you have experience doing so. It is not like cities in the US. We would be delighted to provide you with a car and a driver."

Of course you would. "I may take you up on that too. But right now I would like to wash up and change clothes if you do not mind."

"I do understand," Terry said handing her the keycard. "Call me if you need anything at all."

"I will," Cally said pushing the door open. She caught a glimpse of Terry heading down the hallway away from the elevators, as she entered the room.

The foyer for Room 3 led to white and gold sitting area with a couch, chairs, and a meeting table at the end. A separate red and gold bedroom with a gray and black bathroom opened off the side of the living/meeting room. The elegant bathroom had a dual sink vanity and a raised Jacuzzi tub surrounded by a square of black teak. A tiny bar and kitchen area hid behind a shoji screen next to the meeting area. Each room had matching carpeting and fresh flowers were everywhere. The art on the walls looked original.

This is some guest room. I could live here. I wonder what Room 1 has in it. Richard Branson would be happy here. He's looking for Chinese investors for his Virgin Money venture. I wonder if he knows about this?

***

Calliope called the concierge the next day when she got up. She ordered lunch and a black St. John knit business suit with black Ferregamo shoes for the dinner. She ate her lunch, soaked in hot water, and went to sleep again in the king sized bed. Exhaustion from the trip and the night before it still lingered, even after sleeping until 9:00 am and doing nothing except sitting like a lump beside the hotel pool the day before.

The music playing at the crowded concert in the park got louder and louder when the scene melted into a grassy strip beside a gray concrete building. She was being led into the building by uniformed security guards. *Oh, the alarm. Fucker won't turn off, on the screen.*

Oh it's ringing. Slide it. "Hello. Okay yes you can bring them up." *16:32.* She flopped back on the bed to finish waking up before the clothes were delivered.

The suit and shoes fit exactly. *Damn, they probably went through everything in my house. I am going to have to fix my security when I get home – whenever that may be.*

"Hello Calliope, are you recovered some from the travel?" Terry said when she answered her cell phone. *Another reminder, eh.*

"Oh yes, thank you I feel much more human now. ... No I did not go out, just got an outfit and slept. ... Oh of course I can find it. Top floor? ... Yes I got it. Enter 37842 on keypad in elevator. Is that where the dinner is? ... Okay, I will see you in about 10 minutes. ... Bye."

Calliope could not find a keypad on the control panel for the ultra modern Larsson elevator so she just pressed the button for the "Penthouse 搭連正房的屋頂, 耳房,屋檐" A black touch-panel lit beside the floor keys and she tapped in the code to start the elevator.

The elevator doors opened on a small teak paneled antechamber with a door on the left side with an intercom next to it.

"Hello Calliope," a soft sibilant voice said when she reached for the intercom button. "The door is open, please come in."

The door opened to a simple off-white room with a slate floor and comfortable furniture in it. There were tables and flowers everywhere.

"Do not be alarmed, Ms. Dancer. There is no danger. I have been wanting to meet you for some time," the same voice said from behind a shoji screen to the side of the room.

The entry chamber door clicked shut quietly behind her when she walked further into the room. A huge spiderlike creature with five bright blue eyes over a brutal fanged mouth flowed silently sideways from behind the screen into the room.

Calliope's heart exploded in her chest. She

staggered sideways almost falling over. Her mind seized on the glistening blue orbs. It took all she had to not spin around and run madly at the closed door back into the entry chamber.

"Take a moment, Ms. Dancer. I am not going to harm you. This is a shock, Ms. Dancer. Let your mind think again, breathe, move your feet. You will not be harmed. Are you thinking again, Calliope?"

"Yes. It is ... " she started to say, and then the panic washed back again and she had to fight it to try to clear her mind. Her legs could not hold her up, the feeble things could not possibly function and she must fall over. She felt cold and shaking too, as her mind began to work again. At last she could move, becoming aware of her stiff chest and frozen body.

"That is better, Ms. Dancer," the creature said drifting back slightly and moving what looked like hands on its raised front legs towards one of the tables in front of a couch with a carafe on it. "There is water on the table. Please have a drink and sit down. I wish to speak with you."

Calliope found a memory of herself spilling water around a glass after collapsing on a couch. There was a firm cushion under her and staring blue orbs watching her silently.

"Are you back now?"

Her dry mouth croaked out a yes as cold moved through her, followed by nausea and shaking. Her vision and hearing now connected up with her consciousness and the memory. The room expanded and got lighter.

"Yes, okay," she managed, her mind racing to find a way to explain and to escape at the same time. She pushed down the flight impulse and remembered drinking water.

"You are not in danger. Tell me why are you here."

"Huh? Why am I here! I was shanghaied!"

"Good, you are thinking again. Your brains lock up with too much emotion and are useless until you get them back under control."

Calliope took a drink of the water but could not move herself from the front edge of the couch yet. "Why *am* I here?"

"Because you are still alive."

The cold shiver passed quickly through her and she said, "So you wanted to – you decided to bring me here?"

"Yes. I doubted whether you might be worth it. I wished to know a little more about why you kept showing up in my business."

"Your business. All this here and everything else is your business?"

"Yes it is."

"I have seen a lot of weird things, that's my work, but you are one of the strangest. I still have no idea what is happening right now," she said thinking it would take many specials to get through this. She looked for her purse and discovered it in her hand.

"One of your chemical potions? Yes, they are still in your purse. That is one of the reasons I wished to meet you."

"My candies?"

"Yes. Where did you get them from?"

"I make them. My great aunt taught me at first and then I have developed some of my own too."

"You are a chemist, or your great aunt was at least, then?"

"No, not really. These have been in my family for a long time. They have been useful and are passed down to a few who appreciate them," Calliope said concerned she might be saying too much.

She pulled a cherry surprise out of her purse and chomped it down in one bite. Now was not the time to savor. She relaxed feeling her old self start to return.

"Now that you are more adjusted, tell me why you are here? Why does your work concern me?

"I did not know it did concern you. God knows who would ever assume that. I have a client who wants to know what is happening to his customers." Met with silence, she continued. "His business is impacted and one person appeared to be connected again and again, so I investigated her."

The completely still being facing her over the low table said nothing. She waited.

"Do you understand what you are doing?" it finally said.

"Understand? I don't know what you mean."

"Of course you do."

"He is a client who pays for my services to help him with his business," Calliope said with a twinge of guilt.

"You are makers. You can do more but are burdened with inconsistent minds. Your own evolution limits you. You understand that and why your chemical tools work."

"You have lost me, I am afraid."

"That is of no value to me. Be honest and we might come to an understanding that would benefit us both. If not, it ends here."

Calliope felt the fear come back and struggled about what to say next. It could be the last thing she ever said.

"My client is not a saint, none of them really are. Most humans have both good and evil in them. It is how we are."

"There is no such thing as good or evil. We both know that. Your client is destructive to your social order and benefits from those whose duty is only to themselves at the expense of others. They use everything they touch for themselves alone. They care nothing for the lives nor the actual physical existence of others of your species except as it serves their own ends. Your species assigns *evil* to that pattern of behavior and *good* to the obverse: those who act out of duty to the continued well being of your social web and the others like them in it. My interest in you has basis in your own ability to grasp that. You appear to, but I cannot say for sure. I wish to be sure."

"I am human, I understand the good and the bad in humanity. I have to deal with both of them to do my work. But you didn't bring me here to talk about philosophy, did you? What do you mean, we are *makers* and to be honest, what are you?"

"I will share information with you. It may help you decide."

Cally suspected what *decide* meant, but unusual things had started following her from the time she knew she was not going to be Britney Alexandra anymore. This promised to be one of the weirdest, and possibly the most dangerous of them all. She reached for a white chocolate lemon crème special.

"I am made, manufactured. My makers are like you. They evolved to be builders and seekers. When they reached the point of being able to, they made me and many others like me," the creature went on.

"Made you? You are alive, aren't you? You don't look like a robot."

"I am biological, a living being, just as you are. I am just built for a purpose by other beings."

"You're certainly not from here, Earth then. Why were you made? To serve them?"

"To have patience for one, much more than they. They wished to explore beyond their own world. Even if their bodies could have been modified and machines built to endure the physical voyage, the vast stretches of time required to do so would destroy their minds. I can endure both. Centuries of waiting are what I am for. My mind will be whole and complete, not visited by madness at the end.

"My body is designed, manufactured and malleable. It can reconstitute itself when it needs to, repair itself with chemicals, energy, and the assistance from a few of the maker's tools if I have access to them. If not I can change myself, my physical self, to a more limited extent within a narrow set of design parameters."

"Oh my God. Then you are sent out by they, them, your *makers* to find other intelligent beings on other worlds your builders want to, to visit for them?

Sorry, that's confusing isn't it? Do you understand what I'm trying to say?"

"I understand."

"Where did you start from? Is this, us the first world you have found?"

"I cannot tell you where we began, I am not a pilot. We have visited others too. Some of me and my abilities come from what my fellow travelers and I learned from visiting other worlds. It has been a very long journey."

"Fellow travelers? There are more of you?" Calliope said shuddering to think of many of these around.

"I am the only one here. It was an accident. Our ship had lost too much energy to support all aboard for an extended time. They left me here to survive if I could. I am expendable"

"You were expendable? Why's that?"

"My design had the duty to protect the ambassador and technical designs if they met danger. I am not a pilot or a technical either. I was least valuable on the ship."

"Then the others are like you? They, your makers made them all?"

"Each with different functions and brains to handle other specific tasks associated with our mission."

"Do they all look like you?" Calliope said pointing her hands towards him.

"No. Each of us had simple bodies that could be reconfigured around our brains and sensors to be more fitting with the worlds and creatures we encountered. Those changes take much time, but we are all patient."

"When I came here I was damaged and had little support equipment. I chose a creature that looks as I do now. It appeared to be a very successful predator and defender in a place unknown to me. After I had repaired and reconfigured my body like this, I discovered your species and came to understand my error. By then it was too late to change into a less frightening form for you. I did not have sufficient facilities remaining to change and could not repair what I had, not being a technical design."

"We are not big fans of spiders here," Calliope said with a smile.

"It takes time to convince your species of my intentions when you first meet me."

"What do your makers look like?"

"I do not remember exactly. It was a long time ago."

"Really? You can't remember?"

"My brain is not unlike yours. There is limited volume and memory capacity. Old memories are overwritten as it reconfigures itself and builds different physical connections out of the old connections for the new memories."

"Oh my. I don't believe we can do that. But we don't live as long as you either."

"It is necessary for me. My basic brain functions are firm, but my primary purpose is to continue to exist for as long as possible, to be able respond to new places and new creatures, never, once, or many times. My makers had no accurate way to judge so they made my brain able to reuse itself to some extent as my environment changed and long stretches of time elapsed."

"How can you do it? Don't you forget all those things like how to talk and what things are when you just change your mind?" she said with a chuckle, loosening up and enjoying herself now.

"After all the time I have been exposed to your species, I still do not understand your humor."

"Guess you have to be human for that. Sorry. What were you saying?"

"I have two chains in my mind, consciousness streams," the creature said. "One is like yours and primary, and one is running off from it, but is also aware, almost two minds with one primary. The secondary thoughts can preserve critical memories and perform limited cognition to support the main channel, while the structures building the primary flow are reconfigured as the demands of volume and time dictate. That is all I can tell you with my limited technical functions."

"Lord. So if I have understood you, you are a sane space traveler by design, a soldier design at that, and you ended up here by accident and remade yourself to look like a giant spider. Is that about it?"

"More of your humor, Calliope Dancer?"

"Possibly," she said laughing. "This is fascinating. I've seen lots of things, but nothing like you before."

"It's from your chemicals you enjoy so much."

"Oh, they do more than that. They help me see the world and all the normal strange things in it more clearly. You would be surprised at some of the stuff other people miss going on around them all the time."

"Another reason you are here. You might have something like my secondary cognition produced by your chemicals. It makes you valuable."

"That's a thought. Now, back to the why I am here myself. Why are you removing my client's customers, if I am correct understanding it's you doing it?"

"I need chemicals and energy to operate. They are destructive members of your society. I use their chemicals."

"You *eat* them? For *food*? Christ. Wait now, *really*?" Calliope asked with some skepticism.

"You call it food, it is just chemicals and chemical energy. All living things consume the chemicals of other life to operate and to continue to live. I am no different."

"But these are people. If that's your real reason."

"I am not."

"Wait, isn't that counter to what you are for, to meet other sentient creatures and understand them for your builders?"

"Not always. I am built to survive, just as you are. I can be an efficient survivor and remove damaged members of your society at the same time for you. You do the same thing yourselves. They were also directly interfering with my interests. Two birds with one stone you would say."

"We don't eat them though. The rest of it is interfering in out society. Don't you have a moral problem with that?"

"Whatever I do to your society is just an is. You will adjust because you are a flexible and adaptive species. You build flexibility into your societies. You design them to cope with your own uncertain environment. Meanwhile, evolution adjusts you and your societies to accommodate perturbations, just like all life and all societies everywhere that are successful. Those two things damp out any disruptions that I or any other outsider might bring to your environment."

"Okay fine, but if you bring something we are not ready for and change our historical trajectory in some unknown way, then isn't it a problem for us, and you too sooner or later, as a representative of your builders?"

"If a new disease emerges you adjust, or a war, or a new technology changes everything, you adjust. If I bring something you are not ready for it dies out because your selves, your systems, and your technologies cannot utilize it, or maybe even recognize it through those mediums. Your kind would most likely just assign it to superstition or magic then. There is no planned path for you or any other species on any world. They all evolve wherever they evolve to because of random stresses and perturbations. I am just another random input."

"But if your people, your makers, come and destroy us or you do something to destroy us that is wrong, isn't it?"

"I cannot do that and my makers are never coming here. I exist because they cannot. You destroy your own kind and other societies of your kind on your world all the time. I can add nothing worse. It is *your trajectory* as you call it."

"You are here because you wanted to find out

what was happening to your missing criminals. Now you know. What are you going to do?"

Calliope thought for a moment. "I have many more questions. And I don't kn ... No, I have to know why you think I have value to you, and why do you concern yourself with my investigation. After all, I could be just another missing person if you chose to eat me like the rest."

"I do not want an intersection of my interests with those of your client. It could influence my privacy or the businesses protecting it. There are many people who work for me in those businesses to ensure that privacy, and they would be adversely affected also."

"First, you have to stop *eating* people. You can get chemicals – food in other ways. You kind of brought it on yourself."

"I find it difficult sometimes to alter my nature to protect. It has caused issues like this in the past."

"And how long has it been?"

"One hundred twenty-six years."

"Oh," Calliope said remembering he was built to be patient. "What have you done in the past – to correct things?"

"Eliminated the direct threat. But, your species has much more efficient communications and information management now, and there are many more of you. This time it will have to be done more carefully."

"*That's* why I'm here, to help do that then?"

"Possibly. If you choose to."

"I have to think about it," she said after a moment. Her head was spinning with what she just heard. She reminded herself that Henry Appleyard might be every bit as dangerous at this creature standing in front of her.

"This is not as simple as eating your enemies – what do I call you anyway?"

"I am known as Song."

"Okay, Song. I have to learn more and have time to digest all of this. My client *isn't* just another human being making waves for you and your privacy. Do you understand that, him?"

"I believe I do. There have been others like him, others like the woman in the car you knew. They are harder to eliminate and are of subtlety different chemicals."

"My God, you make is sound so simple – just their chemicals. Don't you see – feel – the difference with them? They are more dangerous, and I haven't heard of very many of them being *eliminated* before this. You really aren't from here."

"Really? My makers gave me a much less troublesome portfolio of instincts than your primitive feelings. Those are just the primordial residue of your evolution pushing you to live, consume other life forms, defend yourself from other life forms seeking your chemicals, and reproduce. Your species places far too much importance on them, most likely because you have not been able to rid yourselves of them. My makers were able to, but you are on the verge now. It will be a huge step forward to improving your lives and societies."

"You just don't know how powerful feelings can be, do you? Don't underestimate them in humans."

"I do feel in the way you may mean sometimes. I synthesize bits of information into a whole in large steps you call intuition. I just do not color it with survival instincts, emotions from older autonomous parts of my brain to make it appear special or mysterious to the cognitive parts of my brain."

"I do accept that your feelings matter to you and are familiar to many of your species, it is how you are and I respect it. I am how I am."

"What happens now?" Calliope asked feeling she had passed his test — for now.

"There is a gathering of some of the people who support my various activities. I believe Terry Carter invited you to it. Take time to attend and think about what you will do now. I caution you though to be discrete. Many know different things about my business and me, not all have full confidence. You will know more than some others may. Your part is different and new."

"You are not worried I will just leave?" Calliope said taking another drink. "I don't yet know what I am to do with all this."

"I suspect you have pretty much decided. I feel it."

She could not tell if Song was smiling, laughing, or asleep, but she suspected he did understand more of human humor than he let on. She also knew she would end up doing what she could for his *privacy*. He was far too amazing to just walk away from. She was also positive Appleyard would be a terrible problem.

Appleyard

Mike Macartney

Chapter 16

Samantha's death had moved Tyrone more than he had realized or expected it would. Maybe it because this was the first employee lost in many years, and Samantha had been one of the toughest. No clear understanding emerged about why, or even what had happened yet either. She had been schmoozing with an up-and-coming politician in Las Vegas, a top cop no less, and then she was torn apart on a public street with him, his driver, and his armored car.

Tyrone waited quietly in the Nationwide lobby for his meeting with the chief. He knew this summons was because of Samantha. Senior employees of Nationwide didn't just die flamboyantly in public unless something more was up. He only got called in like this when the chief needed his direct, relentless talents to handle a special problem, one that needed more explicit action than political finesse. He could be diplomatic with an effort when he needed to be, but he defaulted to a cold-blooded setting when just brute force and ruthlessness served with cold calculation were called for.

Tyrone could remember one other time, when an aspiring member of the corporation tried to carve out his own empire in the Southeast and killed four other powerful employees in the region. The chief got a fixer like him to take care of it then too. He knew there had been a few other times like this over the long history of the corporation, but nothing like what happened to Samantha. No obvious upstarts inside Nationwide appeared to be jockeying for power; this looked more like an outsider was taking on the corporation directly. It happened occasionally since the founding of the enterprise when its charter was first written. Usually a client or employee decided they would like first count on the money and could run it better if they were in charge. Appleyard had been the CEO for longer than Tyrone or anyone else could remember. Nobody had ever gotten very far with him with things like this.

The bored security in the lobby flinched to a semblance of shock and attention when the chief himself blasted out of the elevator and shouted rapid fire, "Tyrone! I need you now. Come, come into the elevator, you have to leave in an hour."

Tyrone blew by the flustered guards and strode into the car with Appleyard holding the door.

"You heard what happened to Samantha, I'm sure. I need you in Las Vegas tonight. There's a car in the garage waiting for you," Appleyard said thrusting the tickets at Tyrone and blocking the door with his foot.

"Wait, what happened? I only heard she died in some kind of accident."

"What! Accident! Wait, those nosey bastards don't need to waste my money gossiping," Appleyard said glaring at the guards. He let the door close and hit the stop button to hold the elevator car. "She and one of our most promising clients were sharing a car when it was ambushed. She, the client, and the driver were torn limb-from-limb and the car demolished as near as I can tell."

"What, Samantha was killed and dismembered? How can that be, she was one of our best – tough as nails and always aware. The enormity of a barbarous act like this doesn't happen to her caliber of employee," Tyrone said faking his surprise at what he had already heard through the company grapevine.

"Yes yes, and it does not happen to the police chief of Las Vegas either – in his own armored car in the middle of town."

"How did this atrocity happen? "

"I told you they were taken from the car and killed. Here are the pictures from this morning," Appleyard said giving Tyrone a flash drive. "This is not even in the newspapers yet. Don't go charging in there no matter if it is Samantha. You be diplomatic Tyrone, diplomatic, then you take care of it," Appleyard said looking up into Tyrone's gleaming black eyes and making *take care of it* very clear – and diplomatic too. The CEO burned with fury, but he did not need a galumphing fool running into something like this half-cocked, or they would have worse than just being torn apart into bits to deal with.

Tyrone felt the cold weight in his guts pulling him away from exploding anger into calm calculations about what his next steps would be. He would be wading into a gruesome murder of a police chief to get what he needed. Much more needed to be learned before he could deal with it the way the chief wanted.

"I see. Do we have people I can get to, to run this issue to ground?" He said putting the drive into his pocket.

"Call George Stapleton when you get there. He's a cop and we have been tr--recruiting him for some time. He's a follower, but you can pump him. He's floundering, so it will be easy. You know how. Now go, go," Appleyard said jabbing the start button repeatedly to open the elevator door.

Tyrone walked quickly around the lobby and took the stairs down to the parking garage. It would be cutting it close to catch his flight.

***

"Hello, Mr. ... ?" the police captain said answering Tyrone's phone call.

"You may call me Tyrone, Captain Stapleton. I have just arrived at McCarran Airport and I am on my way to secure my rental automobile. I know this is a most horrible time for you and all of the Las Vegas Police force. My deepest sympathies go to you and Chief Daniels' friends and family. My employer also wishes to express their shock and sadness at what has happened."

"Why, yes, thank you Tyrone. We are very upset here, and mad as hell too. We're going to get the bastards who did this. You can be certain of that. We will burn them down and every officer will – uh. Okay, I'm sorry. I did not expect you would, your company that is, be so quick in showing up. I just shared some of the very early details with your president last night as a courtesy, since he was a great friend with Chief Daniels. He told me he would do everything he could, but I am not sure what exactly you might be able to do. This *is* a police matter you understand, and possibly more than that. There is not any place for amateurs in this, no matter who they are. Is that clear?"

"Of course I certainly understand Captain. I am here only to help you and your officers in any way I can with only information. Chief Daniels was much loved in Cleveland and was a long time friend of our own chief. We will do nothing to hamper your work or interfere with it in it in any way, " Tyrone said covering his irritation. *Jesus fucking Christ isn't he an oblivious minion. Daniels didn't need to worry about him. Appleyard got the photographs from somebody else and didn't bother to tell me. Just like him. Shit on a stick.* "Now that I am here and you are so busy, is there somebody I can work with and share my information with? There might be somebody from Chief Daniels' past in Cleveland who is involved in this, and I will want to help you find out very quickly, if I can."

"Good, we understand each other I see. Lieutenant Jacobs is the leader of our special operations group. He reports directly to me. He has been on this like white on rice since it happened. I will have you work through him. Only if he has time and this does not take anything away from his own work, you understand. If he feels you're making any waves or interfering in any way he'll send you packing. Do you understand?"

"I absolutely do. I am only here to help and to stay out of your way at all times. I will share any information I have with Lieutenant Jacobs and take his lead on everything. My only motive is to help you bring these monsters to justice as quickly as possible."

***

"Hello, Lieutenant Jacobs? My name is Tyrone and I was asked to call you by Captain Stapleton regarding this vile matter of Chief Daniels. I am with Nationwide Professional Services and Chief Daniels was a personal friend of our chief executive officer in Cleveland," Tyrone said when the lieutenant answered his call. "Oh, I am very pleased you have heard of us. … I certainly would be delighted to meet with you at any time that is convenient for you and when it will not impact your work. … Calling you at this number works fine for me. It is in my phone log now. It is better since you will not be in the office much I expect. … I do have the information you shared, thank you. … Yes, I can find it and will come at 9:30. … Goodbye." *That's better. He's the one.*

"Hello, you must be Tyrone. I expected you would find it okay. It is more private with all the cameras now," the freckled, red haired man at the picnic table on the edge of the softball park in Summerlin said without rising to greet him. Loud adult night games filled most of the diamonds. None of the players or the spectators seemed to notice the thermometer on the shopping center read 102 degrees. Many coolers littered the grass around the spectators who sat on the warm aluminum bleacher benches.

"It was no issue at all. I am used to finding my way around in many different places all the time. I appreciate your time in speaking with me about this matter. I believe you fully comprehend the issues my employer faces, as well as the obvious ones surrounding the loss of your police chief."

"Huh? You don't sound like the others I have dealt with, or look like it either," the lieutenant said looking Tyrone over suspiciously.

181

"Yes Lieutenant, I sometimes get that response, but it is only an artifact of my education and upbringing. Being a trifle formal and clear in discussions surrounding the situations I am called upon to handle can have benefits. Let me assure you, I am very terse and direct when necessary," Tyrone said taking in automatically that his appointment was also a large, powerfully built man with hard blue eyes and tight thin lips who carried one firearm in the holster bulging his shirt on the left side and had a folding knife clipped inside his left pocket. He probably had another gun on his ankle that Tyrone could not see under the table.

"Your company had been good for my career this past year. If I can help you with your problem I am sure it will be noticed. There will be a new chief coming in and everybody will get shuffled, and I want to end up on my feet from this."

"I understand your concerns Lieutenant … "

"Mark."

"Mark. And I will remember to put in a good word with the right people regarding your contributions that will be of future benefit to your career. Now if we might, would you fill me in on what you know about this incident? I have seen the photographs, and yes, those were appreciated and noticed by higher-ups to your benefit I am certain."

"Uh, thanks. I'll get used to you. Let me fill you in. From the pictures you can see the chief and his car were really torn apart by something. The driver and a female passenger were also killed the same way."

"It doesn't look like a bomb from the photographs?" Tyrone asked, taking care to be direct so as to not disturb the lieutenant's narrative.

"No, it sure don't. That has us puzzled too. It was like some kind of machine did it."

"You mean a backhoe or bulldozer?"

"No, like one of those terminator robots from the movies. There were claw marks where parts of the car, like the doors, were grabbed and torn off. It also looks like the chief and the female were killed inside the car, and while they were trying to shoot back too. Neither one got any rounds off. The driver, or somebody else in the front did. We found two .40 caliber casings, but no other trace. Somebody cleaned up and missed a couple looks like.

"How many people were involved then?"

We can only identify one woman who was probably in the front seat. Nothing about the attackers. That's where it gets confusing."

"In what way?"

"This particular person seems to have shown up other times too if we have it right. That's why we think it was her in the front."

"Can you tell me about that, please?"

"Well, I'm guessing here, but my gut tells me it matters. It looks like she got SWAT called on her out in Henderson the night before this happened – two days ago. Man is that all? Seems like more. … Well, Henderson PD called my guys to a drug deal going down at a dump over on the edge of town. They thought they would need us for it, and it was going to be a nasty one. We showed up for nothing except a couple of bikers and a hooker, and this woman from out of town wandering around outside of motel."

"And she was in the chief's car then?"

"No, not so fast," Mark said with a flicker of irritation Tyrone adjusted for.

"Sorry, go on."

"Well, she got sprung by the chief. Was that some of your handiwork?" Mark said with a glare now.

"No, I had nothing to do with it. I have no idea if my company did either. Our employee could have come by herself, but I cannot ask her now," Tyrone said with a sinking feeling Appleyard was keeping even more from him.

"With the chief calling it off and nothing on her ID, I wanted to see what she might be up to. I left somebody watching her just in case. Well, she goes wandering off out into the middle of the fucking desert, and by the time my guy gets his night eyes up she's gone. Poof, nowhere to be found."

"She just vanished?" Tyrone had a sick feeling he knew who this strange woman might be.

"Or he was fucking around and lost track of her. So the next day we look in on her at her hotel, where she showed up somehow, and she loses us on a fucking bike. Who rides a fucking bike in Las Vegas! Then she calls the chief himself according to his admin, or at least we think it was her since we can't track the phone used, a woman caller is all. And this afternoon we get a witness in the Wild Horse restaurant describing her or somebody who looks like her meeting the chief there. Another witness saw a woman with the same build getting into the front seat of the chief's car. Now she has fucking disappeared again."

"Disappeared?"

"Gone from Harrah's, gone from Las Vegas. No car rental, no plane tickets, train, fucking bus, or nothing we can find. Into fucking thin air. We even asked the NHP to look for her on a fucking bike."

"Can you describe her to me."

"Better than that, here is a picture from the motel."

"Interesting. I am sorry she does not ring a bell with me at all. I will ask the home office if they have any idea who she could be. Might you be able to get me a copy of the photograph? Please describe her physical size too, so I can have a complete description to send with the photograph."

"Keep the picture. Name: Calliope Alexandra Dancer, 5'7", 130, brown-brown, thirty-six, from San Francisco from her license at Harrah's."

"Thank you"

"Keep me informed on this. Use the number I gave you. This will need to be it from me. The FBI is coming in on this. They'll run down everything and lord it over us. Maybe they can find her though. I'll touch base when I can," Mark said, staring Tyrone in the eye and then standing up. "Wait a few minutes after I leave and then take off."

Tyrone sat staring at the picture of Calliope and wondering just what the fuck she and Appleyard were up to.

Mike Macartney

Chapter 17

Shanghai China Friday July 25, 2014

Calliope walked into the gathering in the 12th floor meeting room not sure just what she would meet there. Song had given her another keypad code for the room. It took up a corner of the building and looked out of two glass sides onto the darkening city.

One section had tables for a dinner service. The uniformed waiter next to the door took her over to a table by the window when she opened the door. Terry waved at her when she approached. She was sitting next to an older and a younger man who Calliope was seated next to.

"I expect you might be hungry," Terry said. "Dinner will be brought in a moment, would you like something to drink? Tea? Wine? Anything else?"

"Thank you, I would love a glass of wine and some water," Cally said with a dry mouth and a sudden realization she was starved. She downed the glass of water in front of her and the waiter turned to get her drink after pouring her more water.

"Ah, that's better. I'm hungry too. It's been a long day. What time is it anyway?"

"Eight thirty. May I introduce Mr. Fu-Hsi Chen," Terry said indicating the older man, "and this is Mr. Toy."

"How do you do, Miss Dancer," Chen said standing to extend his hand. The young man next to Calliope also stood and waited to greet Calliope.

Terry began after drinks were set in front of everyone. "I will be a translator for Mr. Chen if necessary. Let me give you a little background first, if I may. Mr. Chen has business interests here. He has had some issues with someone whom I believe is a customer of yours, a Mr. Appleyard.

Calliope felt her stomach fall and glugged her wine at Terry's straightforward opening. She felt Chen and his companion's eyes bore into her.

"Do not be distressed Miss Dancer," Chen said in accented English. "Things will be done. We will make sure you are okay, but we need your cooperation. Do you understand this?"

"Yes, I believe I do. Go on please."

"We will begin then. Please tell us about Mr. Appleyard and what you do for him?" Chen said with the same directness as Terry.

"Uh, basically, he hired me to find out what was happening to people who were his customers. They vanished in several places around the world over the last year or so. He asked me to find out what was happening to them," Calliope said after thinking a moment and deciding to be direct, given she had little choice.

"Yes, and what have you found out?"

"I think now the – a person I met up ... – today might be involved. He was in Las Vegas two nights ago when something happened to some people I was in a car with. He might be connected with a woman named Marlana Garcia, the woman who brought me here yesterday. I don't know exactly why it is all happening."

The two men spoke to each other in Chinese briefly, then the younger turned to Calliope. "My uncle agreed that I will speak for both of us," he said in English with an American accent. "I believe your business relies on being very careful with your client's information. We expect you to keep anything about our business very private also. Do you agree?"

"Yes."

"I will begin by telling you in confidence that some of our long term business has been in casino gaming. It's been a bank of sorts for our family for a very long time, from when we were not allowed to operate businesses, or even own them openly because of who we are. That's less important now and the industry operates in a more rigorous manner than before, but it's still a family tradition.

"The gaming business has always attracted less scrupulous individuals, especially in the early days in America when outright criminal organizations owned and operated many large and small enterprises. Like I said, it served our interests since we could be silent partners and everything was in cash. However, people like Mr. Appleyard and his particular customers always wanted more from us. He and they did all they could to get into all our affairs, particularly through the gaming business. I suspect you would be shocked at the places and levels at which they operate. Or not, given who you were riding with the other night," Mr. Toy said watching Calliope's response carefully. Seeming satisfied he went on.

"There's been a little too much open conflict recently. Your client has become more aggressive in his tactics, and we have to be more aggressive beyond just removing one of his bothersome agents now and then."

"So, is that why you killed the police chief, and have been *removing* the others I have been told of?"

Mr. Toy almost smiled. "Yes. That's why you are here," he said waiting for it to sink in.

You mean alive, she thought. *Eesh, they're telling me so much so fast: to see if I get it and what side I'm on. It's a war, that's what this is, it's a war. How'd I get into the middle of this?*

"So you want me to do something for you about Mr. Appleyard," Calliope finally said.

"Not exactly. Rather we're going to do something for you in exchange for your participation, a small assistance on your part. Otherwise you leave to report to your client what you have learned."

"What? I don't understand at all. You're saying, I just leave and go report if I don't decide to help you? Then what happens?" Calliope said trying to hide her surprise.

"Nothing. You will have chosen your own future then. It would then be messy for us to clean up. It would disturb many things best kept quiet. Innocent people would be harmed in the process. But nothing directly to you – immediately."

"If I choose to help you, then what happens?"

"You go report to your client."

"What!"

""Maybe a bit more than that," Mr. Toy said smiling. We will of course, *help* you make your report and there will be much less drama afterwards. It will require you to be *very* cautious and *very* convincing. You can act, can't you? Or you will have to learn to very quickly, but I suspect you already know how. In any case, if you choose to do it our way it should leave you outside of much of the blowback, in a much better place than you would be in the first alternative."

"Then I will give him false information, lie?"

"Not exactly. You will report just a part of the information and we will add a few things to it. Now please decide what you will do," Mr. Toy said abruptly.

"Right now? How will you know if I am telling the truth if I say yes?"

"Does it matter? If you help us and report what you think is true, then the first thing happens and you're responsible for it. You will *probably* live with the choice. Your life will go on, but it might be far less enjoyable than it has been up to now."

"Oh. I see. A Hobson's Choice inside a Prisoner's Dilemma. Take all or nothing and both choices are bad – and there's no getting out of the game. Is that about right?"

"Yes, that sounds about right," Mr. Toy said smiling again.

" I have no idea what this all means yet, but it looks like there's not much else I can do," Cally said finishing the last of her wine and looking at her table companions. "I would like more of this very good wine, please?"

"Of course," Terry said smiling at her, while the two men spoke in Chinese for a moment before Mr. Chen addressed her cheerfully.

"Thank you, Miss Dancer, you will not regret this. You have made the choice that will bring good luck to you."

She laughed and nodded to him. "I fucking hope so, pardon my French."

"It's true, Ms. Dancer," Mr. Toy said laughing with his companions.

"Calliope"

"Calliope. Joseph. Now let's eat."

Joseph looked over her shoulder and tipped his head back slightly to motion to someone. When Calliope turned to look, Marlana was walking up to the table dressed in a black cocktail dress with a big smile on her face.

"Good evening Calliope," She said.

"So we meet again, and again," Calliope said lightly, nodding.

Joseph was smiling too, when Cally turned back. "My wife. You two have met."

Cally shook her head and laughed. "No more surprises tonight, please. I've had my quota for the year," she said to Joseph and Marlana.

She drank more wine and ate a cherry special before the food came. She knew the Chinese cuisine would be excellent, it just would not use enough chocolate.

Checking her texts showed two from Appleyard and one from Tyrone. Appleyard's were the usual, "What are you doing? What am I paying you for? What have you found?" Tyrone's was angry, he was being brief, "What are you up to? Where are you? Tyrone." *Damn all this.*

"Do not concern yourself now," Chen said to her.

"Oh it is just a friend fussing about life."

"Friends are that way sometime. This will not be as big problem for you as you think now. Wait and see." He was smiling, and she could not quite tell if he really believed her. She felt irritated that her face must have given something away and worried about what her meeting with Appleyard would be like, and Tyrone now too. He was probably looking into what happened to Samantha, even without Appleyard's blessing. He would be dogged about it now. *These people have no idea, or maybe he doesn't either.* She liked him and hoped he would not get hurt. *Shit, me get hurt. Right in the middle of this mess.*

"Ms. Dancer, let me introduce you to someone you will want to meet," Terry said. "Carmine Salvatore is a business advisor for Mr. Chen. Mr. Salvatore, meet Calliope Dancer, who is the consultant I spoke with you about. She will be helping with some of the work you have been doing."

"How do you do, Ms. Dancer, I've heard about you. I'm glad to finally meet you," the dark, middle-aged man in the designer suit said holding out his hand to Calliope. His piercing eyes and careful smile met hers at the same level when Cally stood to greet him.

"Nice to meet you Mr. Savatore, but please don't expect me to remember your name, it has been a very unsettling day."

"I have trouble with names myself, and it's been a long trip to get here for me too."

"Yes, I imagine the flight from Florida is a horror."

Carmine blinked. Mr. Chen smiled without a word.

"Oh, so they have given you some background I see."

"No. Now you know why she's sitting here, Carmine," Marlana said, still with a huge smile and a glance at Joseph.

Oh my God, she is goo-goo eyes for him. Old blood and guts. Cally thought to herself.

"I see. Well then we should get started. Fu, I have been arranging the corporate entity in Mexico City," Carmine said to Mr. Chen.

"Wait Carmine, Miss Dancer has had shock and very long trip herself. We have been waiting dinner. It is late. Please eat with us, business can wait until morning," Fu said motioning the hovering waiters to begin serving.

Mike Macartney

Chapter 18

"You're where?" Tyrone said sharply to Calliope when she finally called him back on Thursday evening Las Vegas time.

He had spent three days already in Las Vegas and made no progress. The police had clammed up, and the press mob speculated wildly waiting like hungry coyotes for any new scraps, while Appleyard palpitated through the phone at regular intervals. He had stirred up other employees to meddle in everything too. They knew to stay clear of Tyrone, but still poked around in annoying ways trying to curry favor with the chief.

Calliope had better tell what the fuck she is up to in this, he thought starting the call with Calliope.

"Yes, Tuesday morning at a fucking park in fucking middle of the desert in fucking Bullhead City, fucking Arizona ... YES, by the fucking airport...Okay. I'm really pissed ... I'll be better when we meet ... this better be good ... alright you don't lie, I will give you that and hear you out ... He is being a real fucking pain in the ass and bothering me every five minutes ... Why didn't you tell me yourself. You could have you know ... Yes. I am better now. I have to vent at somebody, and you were the most convenient target of opportunity, seeing as how you did not take me into your confidence regarding this most unpleasant situation ... No, I expect you did not realize I was involved, but you did know Samantha was ... I will wait until we can speak in person then. But I fail to understand why this has to transpire out in the middle of the back-and-beyond ... Yes, I shall most likely have to wait until Tuesday then ... Goodbye."

***

"Now, Ms. Dancer," Carmine began.

"Calliope, please."

"Certainly," he said with a smile. "As I told you last night my job is business and legal affairs for Mr. Chen. I have been asked to perform a few special arrangements over the last couple of months."

"Couple of months?" Calliope said with a surprised look over the lunch table in her room at Joseph and Marlana.

"These things take time," Joseph said. When Mari first discovered you and your, poking, shall we say, into our disagreement with Appleyard, it was a convenient time to put in place some alternate plans. You were in the right place at the right time for that."

"Mari?" Cally said looking at Marlana. "I thought she had some other *alternate* plans for me too, if I read the tea leaves right."

"I did. You proved to be flexible and imaginative. If I have learned anything from Carmine and Joe in this job, it's to be flexible and creative."

"It's how we have managed for so long," Joe added.

"Now does anybody want a special treat after this wonderful lunch, before we get down to it?" Calliope said looking over the group.

"I've heard about your candy, but I think I will try one just the same. This may be a long meeting and it's too early for a drink," Carmine said.

"Then have a chocolate coconut trifle. And don't worry, it helps tell a better story. Anybody else?"

"Do you have something for newlyweds? If you know what I mean," Joseph said with a leer and a wink.

"Oh my yes, I do, certainly."

"Stop it Joe! You're not to have any of that."

"Bur Mari, Calliope is an artist."

"Stop now."

"Okay you two, I'll come up with something for you later," Calliope said chuckling at Joe and Marlana's smiles to each other.

"Now back to business," Carmine said. "Let me explain about money laundering. You may know some of this, but just to put things in perspective.

"Today there is a lot of dirty money out there, money tied to drugs in particular, Mexican and Columbian cartels predominately. The Latin American narco cartels together have upwards of $40 billion in just North American drug money to clean up every year. Old organizations like the Gulf Cartel have been operating since the 1930s, so that's a lot of money for a very long time.

"A current preferred method is to run the money through international trade. It can be in just about anything you can name. A cartel will send money through a middleman to pay a manufacturer, in Los Angeles for example, to buy goods ranging from clothes to toys that are then shipped and sold in Mexico or elsewhere. It includes high-end items like diamonds and gold too.

'The cartels have networks all over the globe from the Middle East to Asia and Africa. The money buys parts for smuggling submarines or Hezbollah paramilitary trainers for the cartel armies, you name it. They are armies, Calliope, large, trained, and heavily armed.

"They wash the funds in old fashioned ways too. You may have seen news stories about Sheldon Adelson, the Las Vegas casino developer who paid a $47 million settlement to the US Justice Department a couple of years back. A gambler from Mexico City, nicknamed Mr. Ye, gambled at least $146 million at Adelson's Sands Venetian and Palazzo. He was their biggest cash customer, and surprise, they never thought to report it, hence the $47 million settlement. When the US let Mexico prosecute him they found another $207 million at his home. It was alleged to be Sinaloa Cartel money. Mexican banks were also implicated."

"I can follow you," Cally said. "I get complicated money stories from some of my clients too.

But what does this have to do with Appleyard? Is he involved with drug cartels and money laundering?"

"Of course he is. He has clients all over the world in that business, and all the others like it. He has been around for a very long time."

"I knew it was an old business, but never thought about it that way before," Calliope said with a shiver of guilt.

"We all get into things like that when we don't think," Joseph said without the smile. "We, our businesses and our family, have run into him and his too many times. He's always trying to penetrate our dealing and companies. We've had to be too careful for too long. It was time to deal with him."

"So all the attacks on his people? You are starting a war with him?"

"We do not want open warfare with him. We have many secrets too, and he knows it. But not all of them," Joseph said looking up briefly. We could handle it but it would be very violent and dangerous for many people besides us. It would not be only a few soldiers shooting up another gang's headquarters. Think about the 60,000 dead in Mexico the last ten years and multiply it. Do you get it now?"

"Yes, I am afraid I do," Cally said swallowing hard. "Messy. Awfully messy."

"Exactly. Sorry to be so stark, you probably do."

"What I have done is put together a company structure in Mexico and in Chile with ties back to a holding company in Canton. The funding is handled through Mexican banks with deposits through Algeria " Carmine went on.

"My God, why does it have to be so complicated?" Cally said.

"Let me explain. The cartels have networks in Asia, Africa, Latin America, North America, and Europe. So do we. It needs to be large and complex for Appleyard to believe it. So you understand too, this is not a large thing for us to put up, and it isn't not for

Appleyard either, by the way. But it has look real to him."

"Really? Small?"

"Like I said we have both been around for a long time."

***

Calliope stepped back on the Gulfstream at 0600 Tuesday morning for the return to Las Vegas. Her head swirled with days of planning and practicing to be convincing with Appleyard. There were a few brief trips outside to the city and she was certain the food had made her clothes tighter than when she left Las Vegas the first time. Only a week from the time she fired bullets down the street out of a wrecked limousine until a smoggy red dawn in China, her normal world had shattered into bizarre shards, even for her. Allison became her escort, cold comfort given what she had learned about the efficient systemic violence of drug cartels, and the labyrinthine web of finance and influence they spun with tens of billions of dollars around themselves. Then there was the dark conductor Appleyard touching all of it with his *services*.

Joseph and Marlana would meet up with her in Cleveland after her stop in Las Vegas for her planned meetings there.

"Lighten up," Allison said watching Calliope looking down at the struggling man made neon flailing at the Monday dawn from the banking airplane. Another fantasy weekend at the playground over.

"You've ruined it for me, it's not the same now."

"Nah, you just see better now. It's always like that waiting for the mission to start. Your training will kick in when you need it and I'm here, and so will be Marlana and Joe and the others. You're not going into this alone. We all have each other's back and you're not gonna get left, no matter what. Buckle up."

Calliope glanced at Allison's tight smile and nodded while buckling in for the landing.

***

"Game Face," Allison said when they walked into the park towards the man sitting at the picnic table under the clear yellow and blue desert sunset.

"Hello Dancer, long time no see." Mark Jacobs said not shaking hands and looking hard over at Allison who came up behind Calliope to sit at the end of the bench from her. "Let's do this quick."

"What's the status, Jacobs," Calliope said with the cold, hard glare she had been practicing. She ignored his reference and nasty grin.

He dropped the grin. The nasty stayed. "I've been collecting info at my risk and ... "

"Just the status please."

"Hey sister, this is my business so ... "

"You're paid for your risk. There's a deposit now and another when we check it. I can stop the first if you want to fuck around."

Mark glared venom at Calliope who mirrored Allison's complete deadpan look and stillness. He did not like silence either and started talking again.

"Justice and the Feds are fighting with us about when to put out that the chief was hit by a squad from the Los Zetas Cartel. Supposed to be for trying to bust up a heroin network and money laundering scheme at the casinos. That's bullshit. They're going to raid some company back east, who they think fronted for Zetas and others to move money and drugs across the country. They say it's terrorism too. Bullshit, so they can pull some homeland security shit and freeze out the department. We're going to put out a press release this week, no matter what about the Zetas and the casinos. Fuck'em."

He's furious at me and shooting his mouth off. Good. Chauvinist prick. "When is the raid and who is this company they're going after?"

"Thursday, near as I can tell. They're all spun up to do it right now. They've probably been getting ready for a long time. This hit on the chief pushed'em to do it now."

"Where?"

"Cleveland I think. That's all I got from my contacts. Big fucking secret."

He's lying. "When are you doing the press release?"

"Friday morning. We already whispered in some ears, and the fucking media will all be there."

"Good. That's what we wanted."

"And so I get the second payment then?"

"No. Next Monday if this goes down like you say it will."

"Bullshit Dancer. Bullshit!"

"Monday. Thank you." Calliope said before he could go on and got up and walked away.

"You did fine soldier," Allison hissed to Calliope walking back across the park. It made Calliope feel better, even if her legs wobbled under her.

***

Calliope was even more nervous on the twenty-minute helicopter flight to Bullhead City. Allison would not accompany her to meet Tyrone, so she wore a microphone so Allison could listen in just in case she might be needed – to locate her body if it came to that.

"Hello Tyrone," Calliope said to the hulking figure facing the Colorado River.

"Good morning Calliope, I am glad we have this chance to talk and maybe clear the air. I have always considered you a friend. I was disappointed when I learned you were involved in my business so deeply, especially considering it was with my boss and my ex."

"I am sorry Tyrone. I've always thought of you as a friend too. I will tell you truthfully, I had no idea what would when I got in that car with Samantha and the police chief. Henry Appleyard hired me to find out what happened to some of his customers and sent me to talk to the police chief in Las Vegas. You knew that. When I came to meet him Samantha was there. That's really all there is to it. I'm not trying to keep anything from you."

"But why didn't you tell me when you knew what happened to Samantha? That is what a friend would do in a circumstance like this."

"I just didn't have time. Everything happened so fast and I had to follow a hot lead right away."

"Which lead you to China right from a bloodied automobile in the middle of Las Vegas? You still could have called me and told me something. You knew then it would involve me, and Appleyard would put me on it. Not that I am inclined to quickly forgive him for throwing me in the middle with no information, but he is my boss so I must accept certain things."

Cally did not like lying to Tyrone, but at least there was a cover story already in place. Her new acquaintances had booked a traveler to Shanghai from Las Vegas with proper identification to impersonate her. She flew at about the same time as Cally's return with Allison. As long as Tyrone or anybody else did not look too closely at the travel times it would stand up.

"Tyrone I am going to Cleveland today to meet with Appleyard this evening and report. There's a Chinese crime company behind this, a big company. They have a network of operations that competes directly with Nationwide. I've just learned this and it's my duty to tell Henry."

"Well, it sounds far fetched to my ears, but you have been honest before. How did you discover this nefarious conspiracy against my employer?"

Calliope played her hand stone faced. It would be practice for Appleyard. "One of Samantha's attackers was killed and I picked his pocket before they could drag his body off with them. He was Chinese and I put one of my private investigators on it while I left for China to be ready for their report. They gave me information on him and his network while I was there. I was able to find out more from a banker acquaintance in China. You know how many friends I have."

"Yes, I suppose that is why Mr. Appleyard hired you. What else can you tell me?"

Calliope filled in Tyrone on more of the details she had been practicing, and gave him a written investigation report on the promise he would not give it to Appleyard before she had a chance to brief him in person – just between friends.

Tyrone hugged her goodbye and did promise to embargo the information until she could deliver it to Cleveland herself. She felt he still did not quite trust her fully again, with a mixture of sadness and fear.

I am sure he'll report right away. He can send it and won't upset the plan. I do hate lying to him. I hope he does not blow up when it happens.

Allison heard it all. Her encouragement and Cally's last cherry surprise calmed her down on the helicopter ride back to McCarran for her flight to Cleveland.

Mike Macartney

Chapter 19

Cleveland, Ohio Wednesday July 31, 2014

Calliope would have preferred to walk or ride her bike to Cleveland to have time to think by herself, and to pretend that things were back to her old normal life. It was decided she would buy her own ticket with her credit card, just to be sure if somebody looked into her comings and goings. She would travel alone without anybody who might attract the attention of Appleyard or anybody else watching her. Calliope missed Allison with her cool confidence and gung-ho encouragement. At least she would be meeting her in Cleveland after the meeting.

Cally had a lime crème on the flight and two glasses of wine. She saved a macadamia cluster for the meeting with Appleyard.

The city looked different now, landing on a commercial airliner under a late afternoon summer sky with towering thunderheads in the distance. The half-hour cab ride from Hopkins Airport to Nationwide felt like five minutes. She felt unready as she prepared to walk into the dreary lobby, made more so by the fading daylight and thin white fluorescent light bouncing off the dark paneling, cutting deepening shadows across the floor.

She waved at the guards from outside the locked doors. One shambled up to the door to talk to her after pointing at his watch and shaking his head *no* at her.

"We're closed," he mouthed at her through the glass door.

"I have an appointment," Calliope yelled through the door with her trepidation turning to anger.

"I'm sorry, who did you say you were?" he said unlocking the door and opening it a crack. Another guard also came up, and a third was talking on a cell phone now. A man and a woman in plain suits got up from the lobby and headed over to the door.

"I'm with Lake Erie Catering. I'm here to collect for the event catering we did for Nationwide a month ago. We still haven't been paid," Calliope said loudly, thinking they did not look like Appleyard's people at all. "I tried to get over here this afternoon and didn't make it. We need to get paid today."

"I am sorry but Nationwide Professional Services is closed for the day. May I have your name and I will pass it up to the finance department," the woman now said through the door nodding at the guard to move off a step.

"Don't bother! I've heard all that before. I'll be back in the morning, and I'll bring my lawyer then too," Calliope said angrily turning to stomp away. They watched her go but did not follow. Walking farther down the street she went around a corner before pulling out her cellphone to call Allison, quickly putting distance between her and the guards.

"Hey you, Calliope, do you need a ride," a strange voice asked her before she could make her call. It came from a large limo driver with his belly bulging his white shirt over wrinkled black pants through an unbuttoned jacket front. He held open the door of a black Crown Victoria that had seen better days.

"Get in Miss Dancer, I've been waiting," Appleyard said from the dark back seat.

"What is happening at your office?" Calliope said climbing in before she could think about being afraid.

"It's nothing. Don't concern yourself. What do you have to tell me? Quickly now, I am paying this driver way too much as it is."

"I have been doing a lot of digging and ... "

"No no no, cut to it Miss Dancer. Cut to it."

Calliope could not really see Appleyard's face or eyes in the gloomy car. Even if he was saying the same things he always did there was a cold, cruel edge in it this time. She knew she would just have to jump in and tell the story with no respite or chance to think. Her practice would pay off now, or she would not make it out of the car.

"I just got back from China. They're coming after you. A company by the name of Nushen Holdings Ltd. is behind the death of your customers. They own parts of casinos in different countries where your clients disappeared, and they may have other crime and banking connections I haven't run down yet. Is that who were in your lobby?"

"Yes. It was them. I'll deal with them. What else do you have to tell me?" Appleyard spit out.

"This is all I could find out up to now," Calliope said handing Appleyard a thumb drive. "It's not much yet, but I'll find out more."

"No, I don't need you anymore. This is enough. You cost me too much already. Good night. Get out."

"But, I have not sent you an invoice yet, should I … "

"Send it to the office. Figure it out. Now get out. And tell that fat slob I am ready to go."

The Crown Victoria lurched off leaving Calliope to wonder if it had all been worth it. The information on the flash drive only went so far, a Potemkin Village of sorts for Appleyard to go after, and hopefully avoid a much larger open war. *I did not even get my macadamia cluster.*

Calliope had a lime crème and decided to walk back to the airport and find a room. The humid summer evening made it a pleasant stroll, even if there still seemed to be something missing. *It was way too easy.*

She booked a room at the airport Garden Inn Hilton, and called Allison leaving a voice mail on her phone where to meet her. She went to the hotel cocktail lounge for a drink to wait for her to call back. She had just collapsed in a comfortable chair when her mobile phone rang with an unknown number.

"Hello," Calliope said expecting Allison.

"Are you in Cleveland?" Tyrone's voice hissed at her.

"Oh, yes I am. I had to report to him."

"Is that so. I need to talk to you. Where can I meet you?"

"Are you in Cleveland?"

"Yes. Where are you?"

"At the Hilton by the airport. I can meet you here if that works. What time is good for you?"

"I can be there in a few minutes from the airport. I've stayed there. I'll meet you outside at the north end of the parking lot. It's where the property ends by the trees."

"I'm in the lounge, we can meet there if it's more comfortable."

"No, I have things to discuss away from prying eyes. Outside. Wait there."

"He's mad again," Calliope said to herself hanging up the phone and dreading the meeting. She wished Allison were with her and called her again leaving another message. "She must still be traveling. Damn." She said to herself.

She had no option except to meet Tyrone and repeat her story again. She hated meeting him this way, but they had been friends for a long time and he would calm down eventually. She wished she had a chocolate walnut coffee tropical cordial for him, but they were so far away in San Francisco. How strange it seemed to think about her safe and cozy home, worrying if it would ever be the same again. She had her last macadamia cluster from her tiny remaining stash of three candies. The macadamia cluster always made her feel better after a rough day when she had to still be on top of her game, but there was no telling how she would react to it now with so much stress. *No other option now.*

She glugged the last of her wine and signed the charge slip at the bar on the way out to the parking lot. She considered telling the bartender she would be outside for a breath of air if anyone came looking for her, but thought there were too many secrets to get sloppy now. She straightened up and reminded herself of Allison's encouragement to be a good soldier.

The humid summer night engulfed her when she stepped out of the end of the cold air-conditioned room hallway. Insects swarmed the lights by the doorway and under the parking lot lamps. The door opened near the wooded area on her left. She stood by the door briefly looking over the almost empty car park. She walked slowly into the shadows of the trees at the end of the asphalt to wait.

"You came," the voice hissed from the hulking shape beside her.

She jerked. "Yes, yes I did Tyrone. You knew I would."

"You lied about everything. I trusted you."

"No, no I didn't," she said starting to shake.

"Yes you did. You knew what was going to happen. You were working for them all the time."

No, I was working for you, your boss, all the time. That's why I gave you all the information I found, so you would know I was telling the truth."

"You set up Samantha. It had to be you. Only you knew she would be in the car."

"Now wait. I did not set her up. I liked her. You know that."

"Bullshit bullshit bullshit. Lies, all lies." Tyrone growled.

"Please calm down. This is very upsetting. Here, have one of my specials and let's talk this through, Tyrone. We have been friends too long."

"Fuck your shit," Tyrone said viciously slapping the bit of sweet away with his claws from her numb and bleeding hand.

"Ow! Jesus you broke my hand!" Calliope screamed grabbing it in her other and feeling the slap of fear and adrenalin rush through her.

"Oh dear. Did I? Well, you lied to me and destroyed my company. They raided it today and said we are a terrorist organization that launders money for cartels, that we sell information. Mr. Appleyard had to escape and they arrested everybody in the building as foreign agents. You brought all this on us and you will pay for it!" Tyrone said in an incoherent growl as his rage exploded and Calliope turned to bolt away.

She felt a blow as her body wrenched and was thrown backwards by her ripping shirt. The violent shock and snap of her head dazed her. She heard a sickening crunch and a wet tearing, believing it was her own body coming apart as she flew several feet through the air and landed on her back on the soft soil under the trees.

"You're okay. You did well soldier. Nobody left you behind," Allison's voice said beside her. She could not turn her head but saw blue eyes in the darkness by rolling her eyes to the side.

"What about Tyrone?" she managed to say while Allison sat holding her head immobile. Others came out of the shadows to help.

"He is dead," Song said.

"Oh no. He was my friend. I'm so sorry."

"He was going to kill you."

"I know. But I would've helped him."

"He was made a soldier. He made his choice a long time ago. It was all he could ever do."

"I don't understand at all. He could've done something else."

"No Calliope, you do understand," Allison said gently, looking down at her. "Listen carefully now. You were in a terrible car accident with your rental car. You were backing out of your parking place. The murderers hit you while fleeing. The ambulance will be here in a moment. You are okay. You were just hit in your car. Now Game Face, soldier."

Calliope heard a screeching crash from nearby and felt herself being carried rapidly by many hands back to the parking lot and placed in the driver's seat of a wrecked car. Voices asked her if she was all right a few minutes later, and somebody called 911 on a cellphone. A man in a business suit was holding her head when the paramedics came to take over.

"Mr. Chu, did you see what happened?" The police officer was saying to the businessman when Calliope was wheeled by on a backboard.

"No, I was coming out of the hotel and I heard a big crash. I saw two men run away and came over to see if I could help."

"Can you describe … " was all she heard before the ambulance door closed.

***

"Have you been reading the local papers online?" Marlana said from beside her bed.

Calliope had been dozing from the painkillers wondering what really happened in the hotel parking lot. Tyrone was her friend then he tried to kill her. She wanted to think it was a confusing dream. It would be okay once she could wake up enough to figure it all out.

"Uh, oh yeah kinda. Allison told me somethin'," she managed to say remembering Allison appearing at the hospital when she was brought in and always being around when she drifted out of the drug haze enough to remember where she was.

"Wha 'bout Henry? He show up?"

"Appleyard has vanished, like he and Nationwide Professional Services never were at all. The FBI held a press conference this morning to announce the breaking up of a terrorist money laundering and criminal intelligence network operating in America. It's big news. They aren't saying what they actually broke up though. I suspect there wasn't much to find at the office. He had time before they came down on him."

"He gone then?"

"Not hardly. It will go on. You know that."

211

"Yeah. I know," Calliope mumbled knowing it wasn't a dream. "Tyrone too."

"You know the rest. There was a murder over by the airport. It looks like a drug related crime. The media thinks the victim was decapitated to send some kind of message."

"Uh, okay. Don't like. He was friend."

"Have the police been in to talk to you?"

"Yeah, I can' know what happen just hit car hotel somethin'."

"Lots of morphine huh?"

"Yeah. Not much pain guess hospital."

"You have an almost broken neck, a broken shoulder, and a broken hand along with severe ligament strains. You must not have had your seatbelt on."

"Oh yeah. Doctor ... "

"She's really out of it. You okay staying here?" Marlana said turning to Allison.

"No problem, I'll fill her in again when she is more awake and can remember."

"Thanks. And tell her her lawyer has been contacted and will send somebody for any police questioning if need be. They will contact you. Is that okay?"

"Yep. I already heard from them and told them to go ahead and send somebody."

"Good. Catch me up when things get better."

"Will do."

Epilogue
December 2014

Cally was getting used to her own home again, making a new batch of candies, paying bills, listening to voice mails, and dreading twelve hundred messages in her email boxes.

Tyrone's murderers had never been apprehended, and she had not heard anything more after giving a statement through her attorneys back in the hospital.

The FBI never questioned her about any files of her services for Appleyard. The media moved on after nothing new emerged about the mysterious CEO of Nationwide Professional Services. She was sure there would be at least one book by at least one national security pundit before long.

Nobody from the Las Vegas police called about the chief, or Samantha either. It was as if she had never been there.

Allison would always be a friend she could count on. Calliope decided that made much of it worthwhile after all. Marlana was a different kind of friend too, if she needed her. She knew she had not heard the last of the *man behind the curtain* either. He would be pulling strings long after she was dust.

"Yes, I'll be right there Jasmine," she said into the intercom for the front door.

"Oh my, it's a fairy. I wonder what this is about? Which special should I get out?" she said to herself going to the candy chest on the way to the door.

Mike Macartney

About The Author

Mike Macartney is an aerospace engineer from Nevada. He spent a career in the space business as an analysis engineer, an engineering manager, an armored vehicle business manager, and a consultant to NASA. He helped to found an IT and a software company in Northern California.

Mike now lives in Southern California where it is warmer.